D0388914

WITHDRAWN
May be sold for the benefit of
The Branch Libraries of The New York Public Library
or donated to other public service organizations.

AUG 2 8 2008

ALSO BY MARISA SILVER

No Direction Home
Babe in Paradise

THE
GOD OF WAR

Marisa Silver

SIMON & SCHUSTER
New York   London   Toronto   Sydney

Simon & Schuster
1230 Avenue of the Americas
New York, NY 10020

This book is a work of fiction. Names, characters, places, and incidents either are products of the author's imagination or are used fictitiously. Any resemblance to actual events or locales or persons, living or dead, is entirely coincidental.

Copyright © 2008 by Marisa Silver

All rights reserved, including the right to reproduce this book or portions thereof in any form whatsoever. For information address Simon & Schuster Subsidiary Rights Department, 1230 Avenue of the Americas, New York, NY 10020.

First Simon & Schuster hardcover edition April 2008

SIMON & SCHUSTER and colophon are registered trademarks of Simon & Schuster, Inc.

Portions of this novel first appeared in *The New Yorker*.

For information about special discounts for bulk purchases, please contact Simon & Schuster Special Sales: 1-800-456-6798 or business@simonandschuster.com.

Designed by Jaime Putorti

Manufactured in the United States of America

10 9 8 7 6 5 4 3 2 1

Library of Congress Cataloging-in-Publication Data
Silver, Marisa.
The god of war : a novel / Marisa Silver.
p.   cm.
1. Boys—Fiction. 2. Brothers—Fiction. 3. Self-realization—Fiction.
[1. Autism—Fiction.] I. Title.
PS3619.I55G63 2007
813'.6—dc22   2007025424

ISBN-13: 978-1-4165-6316-7
ISBN-10:   1-4165-6316-4

228167744
AG

ACKNOWLEDGMENTS

My thanks go to Peter Blauner, for an early read, and for pointing out the way; to Martine Singer, for paying attention during class; to Denise Roy, who embraced the book and ferried it into the world with so much intelligence, attention, and care; to Henry Dunow, an extraordinary agent, an incisive critic, and a great friend; and to Ken Kwapis, always.

For
Raphael David Silver and Daniel Jeremy Silver
and
Henry David Kwapis and Oliver Walter Kwapis
Inspiring brothers

THE
GOD OF WAR

captive to the bright, angry flame of him when I was young, I cannot, even now, easily point to his value except that he happened to be alive for a time through no fault or talent of his own.

The news of the shooting made its way from the local newspaper to the big city papers in San Diego and Los Angeles where it was reworked and retold so that our story became unrecognizable to us, and we read the paragraphs incredulously as if we couldn't imagine people who lived like *that*. The story captured readers' imaginations not because of the boy who was shot, but because of my brother, whose mute, some would say insensate, presence occasioned the killing. What captured people's attention, what had the phone ringing in our trailer in Bombay Beach until my mother tore it out of the wall, what provoked an intrepid young reporter from San Diego to make his way to our overlooked town, was the fact that my brother could not talk or read or write, was more at home with objects than people, and could not look a person in the eye or suffer a stranger's hand on his narrow shoulder without screaming as if he had been branded. He could not, finally, tell any judge or jury what had happened that day to cause such violence. He was a boy locked up in himself. Now there are words for the kind of child my brother was, labels and therapeutic regimens and even drugs. But thirty years ago, in the remote place where we lived, science had not caught up to us, and diagnoses of abnormal behavior, when they were made at all, ran to generalities. My brother was simply "backward," as if he were a sweater someone had put on wrong. It was left to others to speak for him, to tell our story to the police, judge, and the newspaper reporters, who then turned the information inside out, so that the boy who died was forgotten, my brother became the unwitting victim, and I became a hero. But I was not a hero that day.

T W O

1978

We lived an enchanted life in that desert outpost, under the spell of my mother, who conjured a life for us out of nothing. Milk crates were upended and painted to become chairs. Discarded cardboard boxes from the grocery store were covered with madras bedspreads and transformed into coffee tables. I grew up with great physical freedom, which now feels like some relic of an antique time when parents did not believe that adult evils could be visited upon children. Laurel, my mother, could not bear to be hemmed in by other people and their ideas of how we should live, and so I was left to my own devices. I rode my bike day and night, wherever and whenever I pleased. There was nothing more exhilarating than the feeling of swinging my leg over the seat and making those first few turns of the pedals until my wheels seemed to glide above the ground.

We were a mother and two boys: a solitary family of three. We had few friends, and we eschewed rules that conflicted with our privacy and Laurel's conviction that society had little to offer us, but that the earth held much. I believed her without question, not only because she was my mother and I loved her, but because I knew her rejection of the judgment of others protected me from what I had done to my brother.

"INDIGO BUSH," SHE SAID, LETTING her fingers slide over the bruise-purple flowers. They bent at her touch as though they were being petted then sprang up when she released them, eager for more of her. I could feel it on my skin: that prickling yearning, that reaching. I knew the touch of my mother's fingers: cool, smooth, like stones polished by the sea. Her fingernails were cut short because of her job as a masseuse, her hands articulated by muscles so that when they moved, the tendons revealed themselves like the armature of a building, the kind whose beams and rafters look fragile as popsicle sticks but manage to support drywall and plaster. Her hand on my head was good weight. "Prickly pear," she said.

It was a Sunday in late February and we ambled through the desert as we did most Sundays. The rains of January were past, but their consequences, the orange and purple buds topping the plants like the candy orbs at the end of lollipops, were beginning to appear. The desert would briefly come alive with color before the summer heat and sun fired it into an old, faded Polaroid. Bombay Beach, where we lived, lay in the near distance, not a town really, but a satellite of the nominally larger Niland to the south and east. I thought of our community, crosshatched by a handful of dirt and gravel streets, as an asteroid, a piece of something larger that had been cast off and that orbited at a constant, bereft distance from its source. Off in the opposite direction lay the low mung bean–colored homes in Mecca, which housed the migrant workers who dotted the fields each day, moving slowly up and down the rows of peppers and melon. At the edge of our town lay the Salton Sea, the lowest, saltiest place in the desert, lower and saltier even than the real ocean, which I had never seen. That true ocean was not far; I'd looked on maps at school, tracing my finger from the body of water I knew so well to the great, mysterious Pacific. But Laurel didn't like to travel. She said Bombay Beach was a good place to hide out.

"Ocotillo," she said.

She walked ahead of me, tossing back her words as though remembering last bits of advice to give me before she left for her workdays, which often ended long after Malcolm and I came home from school, sometimes after we were in bed. She told me to lock the door and never open it to strangers. She said no TV, no sugar, and don't touch the stove. Those were the instructions she armed me with, information I needed to remember in order to survive her absence, to protect myself and my brother against the world, which she said was full of people with the wrong ideas who did not mean us well.

I watched the raft of her red hair bounce on top of her pale, thin shoulders as she walked. She always told me that my brown skin could withstand the desert heat better than her fair, freckled Irish skin and that I should be grateful to my father for this gift. But my skin was just one more thing about my father that had no proven value to me. Like my last name, Ramirez, which along with my first name, Ares, was an invitation for ridicule. Once, I asked my mother why I bore my father's name when neither of us had ever seen the other. She told me it was important to know who I came from. I was sure that my father, whoever he was, had no say in choosing my name; he had returned to Guatemala and his real family months before I was born.

Laurel bent down to study something on the ground. If it was something dead—a fragment of bone, pale and chalky, or the brittle skeleton of a plant—she might save it and bring it home. The windowsills of our trailer were covered with concave opalescent clamshells, slick as the insides of mouths, the abandoned houses of snails, pieces of wood so pocked and desiccated by exposure that they resembled sponges. And they weighed nothing, as if the sun had leached the heaviness of living right out of them.

Malcolm walked at a distance from us, charting his own path. That year he was six, exactly half my age. I was struck by the fact that this was the only time in our lives when we would meet in this mathematical symmetry—I his double in years. I knew there was something important and fragile about the singularity of this, that something would soon be lost. Even though there would always be six years between my brother and me, the gap between us would grow exponentially greater as I changed and he did not. In my twelfth year, I had begun to have an awareness of the simultaneous elephant folds around his ankles and an oversized T-shirt hanging to his knees. He threaded his way through the creosote scrub, his head cocked to the side as though he were figuring something out, which he was not. Or maybe he was. There was no way of knowing what he thought or didn't think. He made an occasional noise—a splice of a hum, a guttural moan—his private language that I knew was no language at all, none, at any rate, that hid deeper answers to the question of my brother. It was just random and meaningless sound, like the nearly inaudible murmur of the desert; if you listened closely enough you could hear the shiver of air passing through the fingery branches of drought-toughened plants, but you could not understand its message either. Occasionally Malcolm flapped his hands rapidly as if trying to shake away water. Sometimes he hummed. Often he stared at one spot on the ground for so long that I thought time would move on without him and leave him stranded, surrounded by the sea of nothingness that I feared was his brain. His entire existence narrowed in on the time and physical space of one second. And then another. I knew that my brother's problem was exactly this disconcerting habit of fixating on a single, often meaningless thing to the exclusion of all others. But I also wondered whether it would be a relief to be like Malcolm and not have the whole army of my impulses trying to crash the gates of my consciousness at once.

Malcolm erupted with his weird backward laugh, making the sound on the inhale so that a stranger might think he was choking. When forced to explain him to a shoe salesman or a nosy grocery clerk, Laurel said Malcolm chose silence.

He also chose to organize all our records according to the record company logos on the jackets and to pile up books in order of size, largest to smallest, then arrange them around our trailer like literary pyramids. Instead of putting the books back on the grey metal shelves she found in a Dumpster one year and painted orange, Laurel simply used the structures as footstools or side tables for her smelly massage creams and clove cigarette butts, or the small treasures she brought home from her walks; today it would be the dried-out caramel-colored skeleton of a pygmy cedar plant she'd found earlier, which still smelled of balsam when she lifted it to my nose. I didn't know if she left the book piles in place as a gesture of support for Malcolm or because she was the kind of person who didn't kill ants, even when they marched brazenly across the kitchen counter.

Up until that year, she had taken Malcolm with her to the spa in Palm Springs where she worked, and where he played in the little garden outside her massage room for silent hours at a time, piling pebbles on top of one another or drawing in the gravel with an incense stick. But the older he got, the louder he became, and the spa manager told her that Malcolm was spooking the clients and she better do something about it or look for a new job. So, that September, she enrolled him in kindergarten. Within a week, the school plucked him out of the classroom and placed him in special ed. The principal sent home a letter recommending that Malcolm be evaluated by a specialist, but Laurel tossed it in the trash. She didn't want Malcolm to be labeled. "Labels are for boxes," she said, "so you never have to look inside them. You just say, 'Oh, I don't need any more of *that.*' " She wrinkled her nose and waved her hand dismissively as though whatever *that* was had a terrible odor. "He'll talk when he has something to say," she announced, as if Malcolm's critical faculties were so sophisticated that he had judged the culture and found it unworthy of his participation. "Normal," she said, imitating the special ed teacher. "As if being normal is something to strive for."

Laurel stood and let whatever it was that caught her interest drop to the ground, adjusted her pale blue sarong, which had faded over the years to the color of fog, and moved on. I picked up my pace, keeping my eye on the spot where her rejected object had fallen. I wanted to know what snagged her attention for that moment, only to slip out of it just as quickly. Her interests were nonchalant, sliding from one thing to the next the way people strolled aimlessly through an art museum as though they could absorb the paintings just by moving through their rarefied air. But there were only scattered rocks and trampled branches at my feet, and I was left wondering, as I always did, why she loved what she loved, and how.

A flock of birds flew past, their formation changing as they angled toward the sea. I guessed they were egrets, but they flew so high I couldn't be sure. In the third grade, a woman in a ranger outfit named Mrs. Storke came to speak to our class. Mrs. Storke (she spelled it with an *e* but I didn't believe her anyway) explained about the birds that migrated to the Salton Sea, how they used it as a stopping-off point on their way south because it was one of the only unspoiled places remaining for them to rest on the Pacific Flyway. She said that we children should be proud to live in such a special and important place. I wanted to ask why, if it was such a special place, did people leave all the time? Hernando and Jaime Gutierrez were in school one day and gone the next. Teachers were always saying, *Class, this is our new student Leticia, Christopher, Ray . . .* Richard, my mother's boyfriend of the past three years, could only stand the desert for half of each year, fleeing north in his Airstream when it got too hot, or when he complained that things were starting to get sticky, a phrase which I understood had nothing to do with the heat. I wondered if he received some unspoken sign, the way the birds did, that told him it was time for him to go. In the late fall, when the oppressive summer heat finally broke, I waited for him to return with the birds, worrying that he might have found some other place to rest, other people to rest with.

The white students stayed at the school the longest, and so did I, because I was half white, and my mother was the only person I knew who agreed with Mrs. Storke that the Salton Sea was special. Mrs. Storke handed out laminated pictures of avocets, grebes, warblers, and herons. She showed us pictures of the rare birds, too: the brown pelican, the Yuma clapper rail. She handed out bumper stickers that showed a cartoon bird with a speech bubble that read "Keep Our House Clean." We attached the stickers to our desks, and the teacher scolded us for defacing government property.

I continued to watch the birds fly across the desert toward

the water. Their pale wings reflected the sun like sails on a boat. Malcolm lifted his face to them as if receiving the warmth of their reflection on a chilly day. His body swayed back and forth, and I knew that in his mind he was up there with the birds, being batted by the wind, keeping graceful pace with them as if he were dancing a waltz, the steps imprinted in his muscles. I would have liked to ask him these questions: Did he wish he could fly? Would he rather fly or speak? Would he rather fly or be normal? But even if he knew, he couldn't say.

When Laurel was done collecting, she led us back to our trailer home by way of the rubble beach that lined the shore of the Salton Sea. Malcolm's attention was diverted by the tide and the pebbles, crushed beer cans, and bird feathers it brought in. My mother joined me on the beach, where we sat on the broken concrete that had once been part of the foundation of a beach club, when this place advertised itself as a Riviera and had hopes for the same glamour and wealth. I had seen old brochures showing tanned men in tight briefs lifting barbells, while women wearing turbans and impossibly pointy bikini tops lounged on beach chairs, drinking martinis from glasses shaped like their breasts. My mother told me about the famous movie stars who had come here to swim and boat and fish, but I didn't know their names, so they meant nothing to me. She said people had such hopes for this place that businessmen sold plots of land from airplanes to buyers so eager they would simply point down and write their checks. When she told me these stories, she laughed, amused by the willingness of people to believe in what they couldn't see. She was proud to tell me she had no faith in dreams.

Now she gathered her skirt between her legs. The veins on her pale skin were linked waterways. When I was younger, I used to trace them with my finger, imagining I was on a boat, sailing down the tributaries of the Nile that led to the delta of her ankle. I had an urge to play now, a desire to touch her. But a new ambivalence had begun to war inside me, and I knew I was too old for those games. Sometimes I wanted to bury my face in her neck and kiss the skin there. At other times her smell, or the way her throat moved when she swallowed, or how she looked when she sang to a song on the radio made my insides curdle. I was trapped between loving her and another feeling that had recently introduced itself and that I had no name for but that felt alternately like hatred, or disgust, or pity, or worse: longing.

"My sea," she sighed, shading her eyes against the lowering sun. She possessed the sea as though it were another of the half-orphaned children she had collected around her like Malcolm and me, the crippled fragments of the earth she had chosen to keep close while rejecting all the rest. For the sea was a castoff, too. Some sixty years before, travelers crossed the desert looking for a new home. They wanted the land to be wet and arable, like the places to the east they'd lived in before drought and blight made them uninhabitable. Those pilgrims vowed to reclaim the desert as though it had been something else in the first place: an Eden of lush, generous plants and fruits, a place where people were meant to thrive.

Determined, they tried to redirect a river, but the river broke loose and flooded, the water rushing down to this place, filling it up, creating a new sea and scuttling their plans. Laurel rarely spoke about her own past, or the farm in Indiana where she was raised. I knew only a little about my grandparents, whom she left when she was eighteen, and what they did to her. But she talked about the history of the sea as if it were her own, and in that way its story became mine, those early settlers my distant relatives, their exploits my legacy.

"Why did they do that with the river?" I said, testing out whether I was still interested.

"Do what?"

"Change the direction."

"I've told you."

"Tell me again."

"The truth is people don't know how to look at a thing without trying to save it. Salvation is a disease."

"But you got saved. When you were my age."

"A guy who probably got ordained from the back of a matchbook put his hand on my forehead and pushed so hard I fell down. You would have, too."

"But I don't believe in God."

"Glad to hear it."

There was much she warned me of: religion, government, corporations, the way other people tried to tell you to live your life. She did not entirely trust schools, and I knew she only sent us because it was the law and because she had to work. She had no faith in what I learned there, didn't believe it would help me in any measurable way. She scowled when I recited facts I had to memorize for a test on the Industrial Revolution, as though I had been co-opted by a cult and the date the steam engine was invented was some dark password.

I knew this: When she was young, she grew too fast and her back curved like the shape of the holes in a violin. Her parents refused to take her to doctors and instead prayed over her.

"Laga, baga, chaga, maga." The words felt like marbles rolling off my lips. "Is that what it's like?"

"Is what like?"

"Speaking in tongues."

She looked at me, but I could tell her gaze was turned inward, focusing on some memory. "No," she said, finally. "It isn't something you can learn like Spanish or French. It's something that just comes on you unexpectedly, like a fever."

"Maybe they just make it up," I said. "Maybe it's all fake."

"I used to think so but I don't anymore. I think that people can be possessed by all sorts of beliefs, and then those beliefs become real to them. And when those people get any kind of hold over you—well, look out."

"That's why you left," I said, repeating what I knew was the next part of the story.

"Escaped with my life. You have to run from people who hurt you. Run as fast as you can. Get it?"

"Got it."

"Good."

I leaned into her and smelled her clove cigarette scent.

Her parents brought her to an exorcist to cast out the devils in her back. He was a small-animal vet who lived in the town near the farm. He held his exorcisms in the supply room behind the kennel where sick dogs were kept in cages. The vet told her that the devil of lust was sitting on her back, twisting it because of her bad thoughts.

"Out devil, in the name of Jesus Christ," I said, pointing to a spider crawling out from a hole in the sand.

"I never should have told you about that," she said, shaking her head. But she was smiling. She said those words too when the toast burned or if she stubbed her toe, and when her words solved nothing, she let go a hard, mirthless laugh, pleased to have proven her parents and a certain version of the world wrong again. Now she stretched each morning, standing in the middle of the trailer in her T-shirt and underwear, leaning forward, arching back, twisting from side to side. *I'm getting the lust out, boys,* she'd say, laughing at her own joke. When she wore her yellow bikini to water the outside plants, I could trace the bent line of her back with my eyes. Her spine was like a straightened paperclip, the kinks impossible to erase.

The water was slate grey now; the low sun played gently over the tiny ripples on its surface. Malcolm walked a few yards farther down the shoreline. Laurel sucked in a deep lungful of air as if she were luxuriating in the freshness of a real seaside where wind blew in from whole other continents carrying mysterious news. "One day," she said, gesturing to the water with her chin, "all this will evaporate, and you know what will be left?"

"Salt."

"And other things. It was an Indian burial ground once. Who knows what they will find."

"Dead Indians."

She laughed heartily, put her arm around my shoulders, and pulled me close. "You don't take any shit, do you?"

"We could move," I said. "To Los Angeles."

"When you become rich!" She said this with no longing, and I knew we wouldn't move even if we could. The truth was, my family wouldn't have been able to survive anyplace else. Bombay Beach, like all the half-attempts at towns nearby, was a place for people who had a provisional relationship to the world. Mecca, Niland, Wister, Mundo—those were towns of migrant laborers, drug dealers, snowbirds, or wanderers like Richard who came and went with the weather. Daily, I watched Border Patrol cars speeding south along the highway, lights flashing self-importantly, our population diminishing once again as those dark figures in the backseats were escorted home.

"We won't be here when the water turns to salt anyway," I said, watching as Malcolm dragged a blanket of green-black seaweed out of the surf with a stick. "We'll be dead by then."

"Bury me here. Scatter my ashes in this water."

"It's dirty."

"It isn't."

"Things die in it."

"Things die everywhere."

The thought of her dead frightened me, and I felt hollow, as though I were starving and there was not enough food on earth to fill me. I couldn't imagine a time when it would be just me and Malcolm. What would we do? Would we live in the trailer next to this pretend ocean? Where else could we go? Who would take care of us? I knew one day I would be a man, but "man" was just a word like "perimeter" or "democracy"; I knew their meanings, but they didn't signify anything to me except that if I spelled them correctly the teacher wouldn't make me stay after class. I could only imagine myself and my brother just as we were, twelve and six, an unfinished equation without the presence of our mother.

Malcolm struggled to drag the seaweed toward us.

"Put it back, Mal!" I said more loudly than I needed to, but I meant to banish this empty, cold feeling, to yank myself back into the present where my mother was here, taking care, and I was not alone with my mistake. Malcolm's seaweed dangled over the end of the stick like an animal pelt.

"Let him be, Ares," Laurel said.

"He's gonna bring that into the house."

She studied the situation for a moment. "No, not that. That's a living thing." She stood and walked toward him. I heard her explain patiently that the seaweed had to go back to its home because it would die if it was left out of the water. Malcolm's protests were high, wretched sounds, his cry more bird than boy. Laurel created a soft cushion of hushed and soothing words that ran underneath his shrieks as she encouraged him closer to the shoreline. Once there, she helped him tilt the stick. The seaweed slid into the water where it floated on the surface like the hair of a drowned man. Malcolm's howls turned some invisible screw inside me, twisting it tighter and tighter.

THREE

That night, I woke up falling, and even when my brain registered that I was secure in my bed, I continued to have the gut-inverting sensation that I had not yet landed, and that the worst was yet to come. I told myself not to look at the clock. But it was too late. My eyes, those betrayers, shifted to the right, and there was the warning: three-fifteen. Immediately I felt trapped in the night, and even though my mother and brother slept nearby, so close I could nearly touch them if I stretched my arms toward the laminated plywood walls of my room, I was alone. The nighttime quiet dulled the sounds of distant trucks and cars, and the star-pocked sky obliterated the daytime luster of golden arches and other neon enticements. Night restored the desert to its naked majesty. I could hear it laughing at the gas stations and schools, at telephone wires and electricity converters and irrigation canals—at all the human attempts to tame it.

Panic flooded my body, and I sat up. I slid open the window by my bed, trying not to suffocate in the solitude. I smelled the things I knew—the mesquite in the air, the leftover smoke from Mrs. Vega's barbecue next door, fertilizer and ammonia from the farms, the chemical odor of the sea. And there it was: the memory I woke with in the middle of so many nights of my life:

I was seven, Malcolm just a year. Laurel pulled the Plymouth off the highway into the gas station in Niland. Malcolm had just filled his diapers, and something yellow and foul smelling leaked onto his baby outfit. The faded ducks began to look like they were swimming in mustard-colored pond scum. The smell turned sweet, disgustingly appealing, like earwax or toe crud. I slid as far away from him as I could in the backseat of the car but it wasn't far enough and I started to retch.

"Oh, come on, Ares," Laurel said. "You think you never messed your pants?"

"Not like that!" I moaned.

The minute she stopped the car, I bolted and stood on the concrete island between the two gas pumps. Laurel expertly held the baby in one arm. A fresh diaper hung from her mouth like cat prey as she opened the trunk with her free hand. She laid Malcolm on the ripped upholstery and stripped him.

It was late in the day; the warm air sat in place like an old man in a lawn chair with no intention of going anywhere. Those summer afternoons refused to yield; the light lingered until you wondered if there would ever be a night, or if somehow the oppressive heat had overcome nature herself. And then night would take you by surprise like a car horn slicing open silence. Laurel carried a freshly changed Malcolm toward me, holding the befouled diaper before her like a gift.

"I'll take *him*," I said, holding out my arms.

Laurel sighed. "It's just the body, Ares. Everybody poops." She shifted Malcolm into my arms and threw the diaper into the can, where it floated above the rim like a small iceberg on an ocean of crushed burger wrappers and cellophane torn from cigarette packs. Then she headed toward the convenience store. I bounced my brother up and down on my hip as I'd seen my mother do, trying to settle him, but Malcolm grew frantic, looking over my shoulder then twisting himself around so he could look the other way. He began to scream and kicked me in the stomach. I told him to cut it out or else. He put his hands on my chest and pushed himself away from me, and I dropped him.

He went down like a medicine ball. I heard the thud of his head hit the concrete before he rolled lazily off the lip of the island and onto the cracked pavement. He came to rest beside the wheels of the car. Next, the most terrifying thing happened: nothing. Malcolm didn't move. He didn't make a sound. It was as if someone had pressed the pause button on the universe and everything stood still. I couldn't hear the cars passing on the highway or the sounds of the construction equipment going full tilt behind the convenience store. All I could hear was the inside of my head, which sounded like water rushing through a wide pipe.

Then the finger let go of the button, and everything started up at once—Malcolm's scream, Laurel running and yelling things that didn't sound like words, her arms pushing me out of the way as she crouched over her baby. Victor, the fat man who worked the day shift at the store, ran toward us, swaying from side to side in order to propel his body forward, his red company vest flapping like useless wings. He screamed, "Nine one one!" turned around, and did his dance back to the store while Laurel shouted, "No! No!" She got into the car and started the engine, not even bothering to strap Malcolm into his seat, but holding him on her lap, one hand pressing him to her chest so that a flower of blood appeared on her white tank top. She pulled out of the gas station so quickly that the door closed on its own, trapping the end of her Indian print skirt, which waved back and forth as if bidding me good-bye. And because I did not yet understand what had happened I lifted my hand and waved back as the car kicked up dirt and turned onto the highway, disappearing into its own cloud of desert dust.

Later, Victor drove me to the hospital and left me in the waiting room. After what seemed like hours, Laurel walked through a set of swinging double doors. A nurse followed her, carrying something that looked like a huge roll of toilet paper but that I realized was Malcolm, bandaged all over like one of Laurel's homemade attempts at a Halloween mummy costume. When Laurel saw me, she burst into tears. She pulled me from my chair and held me so tightly I could smell the dried blood on her shirt. She said, "I'm sorry. Oh, baby. I'm so, so sorry." I knew she wasn't sorry because she left me at the gas station or because Malcolm was so badly injured I couldn't see his face. She was sorry because she recognized that just like my skin and my name this new fact was something that would last me the rest of my life.

THE MEMORY WAS AS ALIVE to me as it was five years earlier. I could feel everything again: the disbelief, the fear, and that first, nearly imperceptible seed of guilt that took root inside me and prepared to grow. I was agitated and restless. I got out of bed and tiptoed to the bathroom, past Malcolm, who slept on the living room couch. Laurel slept in a room she'd made at the far end of the trailer by hanging strands of stapled playing cards from the acoustical-tile ceiling to form a curtain. I peered through the cards. She slept like a shirt someone had abandoned on the ground, her torso twisted, her arms flung to either side of her. We never talk about the day I dropped my brother, but sometimes I imagined her sitting up in her sleep like a horror-film zombie, lifting a rigid arm, pointing a finger at me, and accusing me of what I had done. Every moment of my life was pregnant with the possibility of her finally saying everything I knew was true. But until that time came, I remained trapped in my guilty life, which was like a suck of air taken in before speaking, a lifting of the foot before a step; it was the first half of something whose consequences were visible but just beyond my reach.

I went to the bathroom and returned to my room. I sat on the bed and stared at my bookshelf, another castoff Laurel picked up in Slab City, the squatters' outpost a few miles from our home where Richard lived half the year.

Even in the dark, I could make out the dull, pseudo-gilded letters on the binding of *The Gold and Gods of Peru,* the lone, stalwart hardback among the shorter, stubbier paperbacks in my collection. It was a library book, long overdue. Two years overdue, I reminded myself, feeling the familiar pinch of humiliation the book induced whenever I saw it there. I had checked it out of the school library in order to write a report. Somehow, I never returned it, and two years later, it sat on my bookshelf. It wasn't that I forgot. I thought about returning it all the time. But the idea seemed overwhelming, as if the book weighed a hundred pounds and I would be required to carry it by myself through the manila-colored hallways of my school to the library, the only room in the entire building that was carpeted and quiet and smelled sweet like new lumber. The book's absence had escaped the notice of Mrs. Poole, the school librarian, and no overdue bills had been mailed home. I was too embarrassed to check out books and face her, so I become a reader of Dumpster literature—books other people didn't think were good enough to keep. I read *The Happy Hooker* and *Jonathan Livingston Seagull,* as well as assorted espionage books with shiny covers. Laurel might have mentioned the Peru book but she was not a curator of the house, preferring to let objects move in and out of it— her desert discoveries, or pamphlets about Indian gurus—as if by their own will, like uninvited but tolerated guests.

I reached over and pulled *The Gold and Gods of Peru* from my shelf. A month earlier I found out through school gossip that Mrs. Poole's son was in prison. Now my crime seemed pathetic. I was an accidental book thief. Mrs. Poole might have been the mother of a killer.

THE FOLLOWING DAY, I CARRIED *The Gold and Gods of Peru* to school, but when I approached Mrs. Poole's desk, I could not bring myself to take it out of my army green backpack. She looked up at me expectantly. She wore an alert, somewhat wary expression caused, I thought, by children speaking too loudly and wrongly shelved books. Most of the children at school were careful around her. Her dark brown hair was pulled back into a ponytail, but one short strand had broken loose, and she repeatedly tucked it behind her ear as though something more private than a lock of hair had escaped confinement. Her cheeks were puffy at the bottom as if she were storing two caramels or some other secrets there. She dressed in shirtwaists and boxy skirts and plain blouses—clothes that made no statement about the body underneath. She seemed like someone who was trying very hard to keep her colors from bleeding over the outlines. The order of her desktop made me feel like I had just shouted in a church. I thought she was too organized to have a murderer for a son.

She eyed me with vague disapproval as if she expected that bad things always preceded good, but then allowed a smile that so altered her expression that it seemed as though another person were hiding inside her, one who only came out occasionally and then ran back inside, as if unprepared for the weather.

"Can I help you with something?"

The sound of her voice interrupting the library silence caused me to lose whatever fragile resolve I had mustered about my stolen book.

"Do you have a question?" she asked.

"No."

A framed picture sat on her desk. It showed a boy a few years older than I. Acne had made a ruddy landscape of his face. In the picture he sat in front of the familiar blue sheet that the hired photographer hung on the gymnasium wall when he came for photo day. The boy gazed off to the left and up as if he were trying to conjure an idea. My mother always kept the photo proof I brought home from school even though the words "Bob Boltz, Photographer. Family and Other" were written across it. But Mrs. Poole had obviously spent the money and ordered this photo specially, for there was no gold cursive marring the image. I had heard kids talking about her son, but there were many different stories. In one, he had murdered someone in a botched holdup at a hardware store in Indio. In another, he was a member of a gang that had been terrorizing towns around the Salton Sea. No one really knew the truth, but each boy pronounced his version of events with somber certainty, the way newscasters appeared when announcing how many people died in a plane crash, people whom they never knew, but for whom they had become designated mourners. The photo on Mrs. Poole's desk sat in a heavy brown frame decorated with painted flowers. The words "For Mom" were stenciled on one of the larger leaves that bent down from the stalk like an open palm. I knew that inmates made license plates. I wondered if they made picture frames as well.

Mrs. Poole saw where my gaze had fallen and her face tightened. "What is it you need?"

I could not make myself admit to my theft and say what I had come for so I went on to my next class, my burden hidden in my backpack.

My botched encounter with the librarian dogged me all day. I had become newly inhibited about most things I did and said, and I wished I had not behaved so stupidly. During the afternoon basketball game, I stood in the circle waiting for big Ernesto and the opposing oversized twelve-year-old center to fight it out for the jump ball. So much self-recrimination welled up in my chest, I had to release it.

"Irritation!" I hissed. "Horrible lack of judgment!" The enemy center's hand reached into the air a millisecond too late by which time Ernesto slapped the ball halfway down the court with his fleshy paw. Later in the game, when the teams were lined up for a free throw, I repeated the word "shame" in a low whisper until it sounded as though the Salton Sea had broken its bounds and was heading toward the basketball court.

After the game, Coach Watson called me out of the locker room. It wasn't the kind of talk that I had seen on *Afterschool Specials* where the coach turned a truant student's life around with one meaningful speech and a slightly-too-hard chuck on the shoulder.

"What the hell were you saying out there? What the

hell is *wrong* with you?" Watson said, and I knew that if I
had just yelled something about somebody's mother eating
worms I would not have had to listen to Watson lecture me
about respect and sportsmanship and how he had given me
a chance on this team even though I wasn't any good at
basketball, but it was a small school and difficult to field a
team and he felt sorry for me because of my situation at
home. He told me I had let him down, and that it wasn't
only me who had to be embarrassed, but he had to be embarrassed as well because of *his* horrible lack of judgment. I
felt the truth of the words like a river of disgrace coursing
through my chest. Shame was as familiar and comforting
as the pillow on my bed, which was emaciated and full of
years of my smell and which I couldn't imagine sleeping
without.

When he finally ordered me back to the locker room, I
kept to myself. I dressed facing my locker, using my back to
deflect the other boys' loud judgments that I was a queer and
a creep. But my attempt to disappear was thwarted when the
school secretary opened the door and called my name. I
couldn't believe that in such a short time Watson had managed to engage the principal in my infraction.

"I'm here," I said.

"We need you. It's your brother again."

If the principal had called me out on account of my behavior on the court, I might have earned my teammates'
grudging respect. Now I was only polishing my reputation as
the brother of the retard. I grabbed my backpack and my
gym clothes, trying to ignore the gauntlet of derision I had

to pass through. I followed the secretary to the back door of
the school. She opened it and pointed, and I saw my brother
crouched at the jagged edge of the concrete schoolyard.

"He screamed when we went near him just like last
time," she said. His teacher called him a flight risk. This was
his third escape in a year.

I set my books on a bench and went to him. He was wearing his customary oversized clothes. His T-shirt fell over his
bent form creating a tent around his legs. He didn't look up.
He rarely registered another person's presence, and I was
used to assuming his acknowledgement. I squatted down
beside him and watched him dig in the dirt. Each time he escaped his classroom he came back to this very spot. I had no
idea why he was digging, or if there was any purpose to it at
all, but the fact that he came to the same place made me
think that he had some intention. I reminded myself that I
was only inventing this logic because the idea of him working mindlessly awoke a guilt in me that was never allowed
too deep a sleep. He worked slowly, stopping frequently to
wipe his hands on his pant legs because he couldn't abide the
feel of dirt sticking to his skin.

"Hey, Mal," I said, "you have to go back inside now."

He did not respond; I did not expect him to.

"School's not over," I said. "We can dig later." I knew I
had to stop him, clean him off, and bring him back inside, but
part of me wanted to let him be. I never knew why he escaped, whether it was for reasons any regular kid would
leave his class if he could—because school was boring, the
teachers were irritable, and the children were engaged in

their own private games of power and torture—or whether Malcolm had whole other reasons. No matter. I was proud of him. His flights were wondrous, because escape was something I knew was not a possibility for me. I was trapped by the very things he lacked—awareness, concern about others' judgments, and by the knowledge that, sooner or later, I would be the only one left to protect him. He was the one who was free.

I brought him back to room 23. The other kids at school cut a wide swath around the "tard room," as if some force inside might reach out and grab them and suck out their otherwise normal brains. Some of the boys made horrible, mocking sounds if they heard laughter coming from behind the closed door, and I had more than once heard my brother referred to as a freak. Malcolm's teacher, Mrs. Murphy, gave me a note to bring home to my mother that said Malcolm was continuing to be difficult to manage in the classroom and if the situation didn't improve, measures would have to be taken.

Later that afternoon, Laurel crumpled up the note and laughed. "Here's an improvement," she said. "How about they hire a teacher who can keep track of her kids?"

THAT NIGHT, I WOKE TO the noise of Malcolm's scream. I waited for the reassuring clump of Laurel's feet to hit the ground, for the sound of the card curtain to flutter noisily apart, for her groggy, soothing voice to urge Malcolm deeper into sleep. But Malcolm screamed again.

"Mom!" I yelled, stumbling out of bed and into the living room. My underwear was twisted around my hips, and I tried to right things as I felt for Malcolm in the dark. He was sitting up on the couch, hitting his leg with his hand.

"Spy, spy, spy," he said.

"Mom!" I called. I was angry that I had to be the one to get out of bed in the middle of the night to take care of my brother. I gathered him to my chest and began to rock him, holding his arms tight to his body the way my mother had taught me to do so that he didn't scratch or hit himself. I risked letting go with one hand, then snapped on the light above the couch. I was not supposed to try to wake him out of one of his night terrors, but they scared me. When in the grip of one, he appeared to be awake but he wasn't. His eyes were open but he did not see me. I felt frightened that my own perceptions would desert me, too.

The card curtain was drawn open, the sweep of it pulled to one side and caught by a hook so that it resembled the way girls at school lodged their hair behind an ear. Laurel's bed was untouched. She was out having sex with Richard. She usually left after she thought Malcolm and I were asleep. I knew she would come home in a few hours, creeping into the trailer thinking I had no idea where she had been or what she had been doing because she didn't know so many things about me, like the fact that I knew what a blow job was and how men had sex with other men. She was unaware of the actual curriculum of my grade, thought I was learning something about American history and diagramming sentences, when in fact I had recently learned how to spell "fellatio" and sometimes I got a bathroom pass in order to lock myself in a stall and jerk off. That Laurel had sex with Richard in his Airstream in Slab City was the only information I held over her, but it was useless as any kind of bargaining chip because if I told her that I knew she would simply smile and ruffle my hair. She was not like TV mothers who ferociously guarded their children against the realities of the body and the strange and sometimes unsightly acts it performed. She walked around the trailer in her underwear and peed with the bathroom door open.

During his terrors, Malcolm was somehow more present than he ever was during the day. He looked at me as though he was about to say something, maybe even explain what he had been thinking about all his life. But I knew not to make the mistake of hoping. Hope was only a selfish desire to escape the misery of my culpability, and I knew from reading *Twelve Angry Men*, which I found in the trash outside the library because some kid had crossed out "Angry" and replaced it with "Horny," that I could not be found innocent; the evidence was stacked against me.

"Spy, spy, spy," he repeated.

"There are no spies in here," I said, rocking my brother, although it was unlikely that he was actually talking about a spy. I was used to taking his sounds and gestures and inventing logic around them. That is what my mother and I did: we created Malcolm's world for him and pretended we were right. "He wants juice," Laurel would say if he smacked his lips in the direction of the refrigerator, if the day was especially hot, or if she happened to be thirsty herself. But what if she was wrong? What if Malcolm wanted the opposite of juice? What if he didn't want at all? What if the fall had knocked desire right out of him?

His body changed from being a heavy lump in my arms into something stiff with the architecture of will, and I knew that the terror was over.

"Hey man," I said. He looked toward Laurel's room. "She's not here now." He whimpered. "You had a dream." I was certain this was wrong. The terrors were not dreams, not even nightmares. They were more like the moment when a cartoon character ran off a cliff before he started to fall; they were a seizure of understanding. I believed that during those nocturnal episodes my brother realized that he was trapped by useless fixations, by the need to make the sound "ba" over and over again, or to count peas. I thought that if I were in his situation I'd be frightened all the time. But I knew that in order to have fear you had to care about things never changing from the safe and predictable way they were, and it was not Malcolm who cared about this, but me. So it turned out that Malcolm was lucky. I was the one who was scared to death.

In many ways I was envious of my brother. He could move through a crowd of people without touching anybody like a falcon darting through a forest at full speed, never getting snagged on a branch or crashing into a tree trunk. Some days, I would try to see how long I could go without the feel of another person on my skin. On those mornings, I woke up, dodged my mother's pets and adjustments, her hand running up my back or along the line of my jaw as if I were one of her beloved desert plants. At school I tried to walk the halls without brushing up against another person. When my teachers passed back homework I was careful to take the paper without touching their hands. But after half a day of this physical abstinence, my body craved contact so that almost without realizing it I would move into the path of an oncoming student in the hallway, or sit too close to someone during lunchtime, suffering his derision just to rid myself of that terrible feeling of isolation. How did Malcolm do it? Malcolm who needed everything needed nothing.

He fell asleep in my arms. I laid him down and tucked the sheets around him. Then I made my customary rounds to check that the oven was off and the door locked. I checked each more than once because sometimes, when I was alone and nervous, I believed it was possible for air to move an oven knob or for some strange force to unlock the door. Safety seemed like a slippery thing, something that was there one moment, and then not.

Headlights washed over the house, brightening the windows, and the sound of tires crunching on the rubble driveway swelled, then stopped. The car engine cut out, and the trailer fell into darkness again. The engine ticked gently as the driver's-side door made its customary squeal. I snapped off the light over Malcolm's couch and ran into my bedroom just as Laurel entered the trailer. She barely made a sound. I imagined her holding her suntanned huaraches to her chest, tiptoeing past Malcolm so as not to disturb what she imagined was his eventless sleep. I considered calling out, letting her know that I was on to her and that she had not been there to take care of Malcolm when he needed her most. But there was nothing to be gained by trying to pin blame on my mother; fault would eventually redound to me. The card curtain made a noise like a thousand tumbling dominoes as she let it fall from its hook.

FOUR

After school the next day, I picked up Malcolm in room 23. When I opened the door, the room felt strange. It was too warm for one thing and slightly muzzy; I felt as though I were looking through a camera lens that had not been adjusted to focus. A boy in a wheelchair hung his head over his desk in a way that did not resemble either concentration or sleep. In one corner Mrs. Murphy led a group of kids in a song that sounded like "Twinkle, Twinkle" only the words were stretched out like Silly Putty—"star" became "staaaaah"— and the tune wandered erratically like a wind-blown plastic bag. Malcolm sat at a desk counting paper clips and putting them into piles. I told Mrs. Murphy I had to take him to the dentist.

"Doesn't your mother take you to your appointments?" she said.

"No."

She nodded, her grey bob swinging around her jaw, as if adding this information to a growing list in her head.

We waited for two hours at the free clinic. Malcolm was

content sitting on the floor of the waiting room, fingering old copies of *Ranger Rick*. He made some of his sounds and shook his hands in the air until I wiped off Magic Marker stains he'd gotten on his fingers at school. Kids stared openly at him, but this bothered me less than the parents, who pretended not to notice but drew their children to them protectively and rearranged their sitting positions so that they no longer faced us as if they meant to erase us by looking away. Finally, a nurse called our names. She led us into another room where eight chairs were lined up side by side, all but two of them filled with open-mouthed patients. Dentists and assistants in white circled the chairs like bees.

"We'll do you both at the same time," she said, her nylon thighs swishing together under her white uniform as she led us to the available chairs.

"One at a time would be better," I said.

"Better for who? We have a waiting room full of people."

I was angry with my mother for not having taken care of this problem when she made the appointments. But she never thought about the difficulties Malcolm faced in the world. She ignored them or didn't see them or chose to deny their possibility because to do otherwise would have meant accepting the fact that Malcolm was strange.

"He can't do it unless I'm with him," I said.

"Look, a lot of kids are scared of the dentist," the nurse said, checking her watch. "But we have prizes! Don't you want a prize?" She smiled as if she remembered she was supposed to, and I noticed her teeth were yellow, a fact that emboldened me, as if her inability to benefit from her own science indicated an overall weakness. She brought her hand toward Malcolm's back, and I made a silent decision to let her suffer the consequences. When she touched him, he shrieked as I knew he would, and she jumped back, her face coloring with embarrassment at having caused such a reaction in front of her colleagues. I had won; she would do anything to get Malcolm to calm down. I would get my way without having to say anything about what was wrong with my brother, something I could never explain to anyone's satisfaction since my mother forbade me to speak about him as damaged in any way.

"Alright," the nurse said, trying to compose herself and relocate her condescension. "Next time tell your mother not to schedule the appointments together or we'll have to charge her for the time."

"But it's a free clinic," I said, worried that this would cost money we didn't have.

"We have a schedule to follow," she said evasively. "We're going to have to push someone else back now."

"But don't charge us, okay?"

She regarded me for a moment. "You're responsible. I wish my kids were responsible like that."

I helped Malcolm into the chair. During the whole time the dentist cleaned and checked his teeth, I stroked his palm and whispered into his ear. Malcolm held his body rigid. His eyes were wide with terror, and he began to hum. So I did what I always did in these situations: "One, two, three, four, five . . . ," I whispered, counting to twenty, and then I started over again.

By the time we left the office, the sun had lowered to the level of the distant mountain peaks. The air felt exhausted as if it had finally given up its day work and had flung its spent self across the land. The low half-light made everything stand out as if the features of the landscape were cardboard cutouts. The coolness was energizing, and I resisted going home, knowing the letdown I would feel when we arrived to find the parking space in front of our trailer empty. I would have to entertain Malcolm, feed him, bathe him, and put him to bed. I'd have to make sure the stove was off and the doors were locked. I'd have to wait for my mother to come home from work until I felt safe.

"Let's ride," I said to Malcolm. "Fast, fast."

Malcolm wore a wide, weird grin as he pedaled, his bike swinging from side to side like it was performing an unaccompanied square dance. "Make no sound," I whispered, pulling up next to him. "The enemy has ears like bats." In my fantasy I was leading the troops against a small village in France where there were reports of Nazi sightings. Having been dropped by parachutes in the dead of night, Malcolm and I nimbly and silently made our way to a run-down jumble of farm buildings whose coordinates matched those on the radio message I had decoded with unparalleled skill. I stopped my bike by the side of the road and picked up two sticks to use as guns for our game. I gave one to Malcolm then pointed my own into the distance and made a firing sound. Malcolm pointed his gun lazily. He didn't know what a gun was or what it was meant for, but I could always count on his skills as a mimic so I was satisfied when he copied my firing sounds with perfect accuracy. We rode on. Malcolm was unaware of his participation in the scenario I had cribbed from a movie on TV. But the very useful thing about my brother was that even if he did not actually understand the role I cast him in, the blank slate of his nature made him the perfect coconspirator. He never tried to change the rules midstream the way other boys did, stopping everything dead in its tracks to assert their own notion of how things should go. And of course he never said the wrong thing, undermining my plan and forcing me to incorporate dialogue that didn't fit my version of events. Malcolm was simply there like an action figure I could move around and give language to.

"Quick! They're escaping! Charge!" I cried, standing up on my bike and peddling as fast as I could. "Draw your gun!" But he had dropped his stick somewhere behind us.

We rode past the old marine checkpoint station. It was abandoned, but a beer can stood on the window ledge of the guard box. I knew that kids came out here to drink and get high and that every so often the police did a sweep. As a result, we might see a filmstrip in health class about the perils of drug addiction, which would show men slumped in alleyways of cities we didn't recognize and dirty-looking hippies who had clearly lost their minds. Malcolm and I continued over the sand- and rubble-strewn road until we reached Slab City, the decommissioned base where snowbirds in RVs stayed every winter and other people lived year round in renegade homes built out of corrugated metal or trailers, all constructed atop the forsaken concrete foundations of barracks that no longer existed. I loved to imagine World War II marines preparing for North African missions in the desert so near my house. Now the only remnants from that time were the dirt and sand-covered slabs and the feeling of something missing. In the distance stood the Chocolate Mountains, their toothy shapes fired to a dusty pink by the late-afternoon sun.

We rode past the bar and a sign advertising a community talent show, past the trailer that served as the church and one that belonged to the unofficial mayor, who also ran the local shortwave radio broadcast. A sitting area had been set up outside this trailer with a handful of mismatched lawn chairs, a plastic table, and some browning potted palms. Empty plastic water jugs were scattered about, some reconceived as planters or dog food bowls. Slab City's residents had to bring in their own water and get rid of their own garbage because Slab City wasn't really a city. It was a place for people who liked to get away with things.

The hard-packed sand around the trailers was scarred with wheel ruts and decapitated plants that had not given up on living. A few people lingered outside their homes, but they did not look up as Malcolm and I rode past. Most residents of Slab City were alone for a reason and they wanted to keep it that way. I pounded on the door of Richard's Airstream, a tube of aluminum, its surface a patchwork of cast-off material that Richard cobbled together whenever the trailer needed repairs. He appeared at the door, stooping to fit his long, narrow body inside the frame. He wore a faded work shirt and blue jeans. His freshly shaven head revealed two thick blue veins that ran behind his ears, paralleling the temples of his round, rimless glasses. His skin was baked brown and hard by the sun. A tattoo of a Chinese dragon snaked up his forearm. Malcolm screeched.

"You yell like that, someone's liable to come out of their trailer and shoot you," Richard said, though I knew he enjoyed Malcolm's enthusiasm. Richard was in the army during Vietnam but he said things like "ancient history" or "worn-out story" whenever I asked about his time there. For a while I was convinced that he worked for the CIA, but Laurel told me she didn't think Richard was someone a government would trust. He was, however, the only person outside of my family whom Malcolm would allow to touch him, and now Malcolm pulled on his arm.

"Okay, okay," Richard said. "But I'm not paying this time. Business is bad."

"No fair," I said, disappointed. One of the things I looked forward to most about Richard's arrival each of the past three years was the fact that he allowed us to go scrapping with him in the dirt fields near Slab City, where bullet casings and pieces of shrapnel and the occasional bomb fin turned up from a time when the marines used the place as a training ground. Usually Richard rewarded our finds: a nickel for small scraps, a quarter for something big like an alloy casing. He told us you could still find entire bombs in the farthest fields that abutted the mountains some forty miles away, land that was still used by the military to stage air raid drills, but he never took us all the way out there. There were times when I could see the mushroom clouds of a bomb explosion from that faraway base, and when I did, my chest welled up with the excitement and fear of danger so close at hand. Even though the war in Vietnam was over, I knew from the constant sound of distant artillery that the idea of war was never fully laid to rest. I understood that there were always people plotting and preparing, that there were always enemies.

"*Mi amigo's* not doing much business these days," Richard said, referring to the Mexican junker who bought his finds then turned around and sold them to a foundry in Tijuana. "The price of aluminum is way down. I don't get paid, you don't get paid."

"Come on," I complained.

"That's my deal," he said. "Take it or leave it." His voice was always low and soft, making it seem that he was somehow farther away from us than he actually was. I had never seen him angry, even when I pestered him with questions about the war, or when Malcolm had a tantrum. But I was never fully at ease with him either because I felt that the effort it took for him to suppress the caged roar that rumbled beneath his voice was great and that he could not support it indefinitely. There was some dormant power I sensed residing within his stiff, upright posture, a tension behind his always alert gaze. He patrolled his surroundings from left to right without turning his head like a warning beacon. He barely nodded to signal assent as if too much movement would betray him. I tortured myself wondering whether or not he had killed someone in the war, but I knew I should never ask. Like me, I felt he was a bearer of secrets, and this made my time with him exquisitely charged.

Malcolm loved the bumpy ride in Richard's open-roofed Jeep over the rock dunes. We lurched forward and back, flying over boulders and in and out of the washes that had been carved into the desert floor by ancient rivers. Richard huffed and groaned, his cigarette bobbing between his lips. He made a big show of effort as he worked the vibrating gearshift. The long fingers of his left hand gripped the frayed plastic coating of the steering wheel so hard that his knuckles were white. I imagined the wheel was the neck of a Vietcong soldier and knew that man would be dead by now.

When Richard stopped the Jeep, Malcolm and I scrambled out. "What's yours is mine!" Richard called after us. He threw a beat-up cowboy hat onto his head, took his metal detector out of the back of the Jeep and began to walk slowly, making wide arcs with the machine. It gave off a soft, steady hum. I was never sure Malcolm understood what we were looking for; he eagerly presented rocks and pull tabs from soda cans to Richard as if each were an important find. Sometimes he just wandered, and I knew he wasn't looking for anything at all.

I dragged my feet to displace the top layer of soil. Without the incentive of cash, I considered giving up the whole search. But the truth was that I loved studying the ground, directing my gaze over minute bits of earth as they passed below me. My breath steadied to a constant rhythm, and my body relaxed. When I was scrapping with Richard, I didn't think about Malcolm or what I had done to make him the way he was. I didn't worry about what Laurel thought when she looked at me or about my overdue library book, or Coach

Watson's disappointment. I thought about dirt. The desert ceased to be the impervious, dry expanse I knew it to be. It became a miniature world with its own tiny valleys and mountains, square inches of variegated detail. It became a place where I could never be sure what something was, where there were possibilities instead of consequences. A door opened in my mind and I was in Egypt, discovering a never-before-seen tomb, treasures fully intact. Room after room unfolded off claustrophobic passages, chambers filled with so much gold and so many winking jewels that my hired man, Malcolm, our Egyptian guide, Richard, and I had to shield our eyes. I found two long sticks to serve as rifles and slipped one into Malcolm's hand.

"Cover me," I said. "We might surprise some tomb robbers."

Twenty yards from the Jeep, Richard's detector sent up a strong, insistent beep. I backed out of my fantasy and ran alongside Malcolm to where Richard crouched, studying something on the ground. He held up a magazine clip. "This is a good one," he said. "Haven't found something out here for months."

"I thought they didn't practice here anymore."

"The military isn't the only one interested in guns. You got your speed freaks, your gangs . . ." He turned the clip over, admiring it, then handed it to Malcolm, who cradled it to his chest.

"He thinks it's something to love," I said.

"He wouldn't be the first person to love a gun, that's for sure."

"Mom says it's okay, the stuff he does," I said carefully. I was never sure if Laurel had told Richard about my dropping Malcolm. "She doesn't think anything is wrong with the way he is," I continued, creeping up on a confession I was not sure I was ready to make.

Richard stood up, grunting as his muscles stretched. "Well, your mother . . . now . . . It's like how you never see yourself grow taller. Other people have to tell you what's what."

I wanted to ask what *was* what, but I knew I wasn't strong enough to weather the consequences of exposing my mistake. If Richard had been at the gas station that day he might have punished me. Or maybe if Richard had been there, he would have caught Malcolm. He might have saved us all.

An hour later, Malcolm and I had found nothing. Richard had found some bullet casings and random pieces of metal. After throwing his finds into the back of the Jeep, he squatted down by the front wheel and lit a cigarette. He took off his hat and cleaned the sweat from the top of his head, judged the moisture on his palm, then wiped his hand on his jeans. Malcolm picked up the metal detector and walked with it, waving it over the ground. It was turned off, but Malcolm made the sound of the motor and then such a perfect replication of the beep of discovery that Richard and I both looked up expectantly.

"He should put that talent to good use," Richard said, exhaling smoke.

"How?"

He shrugged. "Decoy. He could make a person think

something was there that wasn't. He could throw people off the scent."

"Is that what they did in the war?" I asked, eager to fit this piece of information into the mystery of Richard. But before he could answer, Malcolm ran back to the Jeep, grinning. Richard reached into his pocket and pulled out a couple of dollar bills. He gave one to each of us.

"You said you weren't paying," I said.

"This is for keeping me company."

MALCOLM AND I SPENT OUR money as soon as we could. On the way home, we turned our bikes into the parking lot of Akbar's Date Farm. Only a few cars were parked in front of the small food and gift shop at this late hour of the afternoon—tourists collecting their prepackaged dates for the trip home. The palm groves spread out behind the store. The bushy-headed trees were lined up in perfect rows like Las Vegas dancers I'd seen on television ads. Inside the store, I ordered a milkshake from the girl behind the counter. She looked like a drawing in Laurel's Indian sex book that I used to read when she wasn't home until it became the foundation layer of one of Malcolm's pyramids. The girl had dark eyes rimmed with black pencil, and her mouth was full and turned up at the ends. Another girl washed dishes at a sink. Her back was to me, and her hip-hugger pants eased down so that I could see where that mysterious road that separated the cheeks of her butt began. I imagined her as one of those colorful *Kama Sutra* drawings, her hands held in awkward dancing positions while a man with an improbably large penis and kohl-lined eyes stood behind her, leering as if he meant to kill her in some disturbing fashion. My groin stirred. I inched closer to the counter and rubbed myself against it. The girls said something to each other in Spanish, then burst into laughter. I grew hot and flushed, certain they were talking about me and my hard-on. But when I paid for the shake and asked for an extra cup, the girls didn't even look at me. I walked away from the counter holding the cups awkwardly in front of my pants, humiliated by the fact that they probably weren't talking about me at all. In five minutes they wouldn't even remember I had been there. All year long, I had been overwhelmed by the new possibilities of my body, but as exciting as these were, they also served to highlight my complete insignificance. Girls took no notice of me. It was as though I were a rumbling volcano that even nearby villagers ignored.

Malcolm waited outside at a picnic table, ripping a paper napkin into small bits. I poured some of my shake into the empty cup and covered it with a lid. "Half for you, half for me," I said, when I handed him the shake and blew the paper off the straw, to his delight. The paper skittered along the tabletop and then fell onto the ground, and he collected it and held it to his face, rubbing it against his skin as if it were soothing. After what happened inside the store, I lost my interest in the drink, but Malcolm was stunned into a frozen pleasure by his. He didn't take his mouth from the straw the entire time he sucked, not even to breathe. There was no end to his appetite. He ate whenever food was offered to him even if he had just finished a huge meal. Laurel and I learned to tell him when he was done eating and we were expert at distracting him so that he could tear his mind away from the food and land on a new obsession for a while. More than any other of his traits, this hunger upset me, made me feel unaccountably mournful. It filled me with a great nostalgic sadness for lost things, the way a rich person might feel if he had to live as a pauper, always remembering the fancy cars and clothes of a bygone life. Malcolm reached the bottom of his shake with a wet slurp, finally taking his mouth from his straw and inhaling a laugh. He peeled the plastic lid off the cup and licked the underside. He chanted, "Be, be, be, be."

"No more," I said.

The shop girls left the building, their fringed bags swinging at their hips, aprons folded in their hands. I watched them get into a black Camaro as I took Malcolm's cup from him and tossed it into the nearby garbage can. He screeched and raced to retrieve it. Cradling the cup as if it were a hurt bird, he wiped off the dirt. He made a soft noise that sounded like "pop, pop, pop," and I knew he was talking to the cup. He would bring the cup home and add it to the menagerie of inanimate objects—rocks, sticks, empty envelopes, and the cardboard cores of toilet paper rolls—he collected and sometimes spoke to in murmurs and squeaks.

On the way home, we pedaled side by side. A flock of pelicans passed nearby as they made their low flight toward the sea. We stopped and watched. Malcolm sucked in a gasp of air and his body grew rigid with excitement. The birds were oblivious to everything around them, bent as they were on their single intention, which was to gain the sea. I imagined them as a unit of elite soldiers executing an order, faces set, minds numb to any deterrent. I wondered what Malcolm thought when he watched the birds he loved. Did he imagine himself up there in formation with them, their single-mindedness of a piece with his own? Was he drawn to the sea as they were, as if pulled to it by a spell, knowing that there he could play and survive and no one would hurt him?

"Do it, man," I said, encouragingly. "Go ahead and do it." And Malcolm let out a caw that was so exact, so piercingly beautiful that I felt the muscle of my heart tighten inside my chest.

LAUREL WAS HOME BY THE time we arrived.

"What did he eat?" she said, as Malcolm bounded up the trailer steps screeching his uncanny pelican caw. Once inside, he spun around the living room, his arms spread out to either side of him. He knocked a lamp off a table.

"A shake," I said.

"A *milk* shake?" she said, incredulous. "With all that sugar? Why would you do that?"

Malcolm spun into one of his book pyramids. A metal ashtray flew off the top and clattered against the wall. Butts and ashes fell to the ground.

"He liked it," I said, trying to defy the obviousness of my poor judgment. "Why can't he have things he likes?"

But she was too busy with him to bother with my petty

rebellion. I retreated to the opposite side of the room. Laurel waited for the right moment to step in and grab Malcolm, the way girls at the school playground waited to leap into the path of the double Dutch ropes. She reached for his shoulder, but he eluded her. When she finally caught hold of his shirt, she drew him to her and wrapped him in her arms. He squawked and continued to try to twirl, but she had him trapped.

"Let's have a good hot soak, my little bird," she said into his hair as she moved him awkwardly toward the bathroom. "Ares, help out here!"

Reluctantly, I followed. The bathroom was small, and with all three of us in there and Malcolm out of control, I could barely move. As Laurel bent down to run the bathwater, I took a fistful of his T-shirt in my hand. "Arms up," I said. He grinned and laughed his odd laugh. "Arms up, man," I said more forcefully.

"Don't get mad at *him*," she said over the sound of water slapping against the tub. "It doesn't help."

I finally lifted the shirt over his head then started on his jeans. When I leaned over to get the snap, Malcolm draped his body over my back, making it nearly impossible for me to move. Finally, I managed to yank his pants to his ankles only to realize I'd forgotten to remove his shoes. Frustrated, I pushed him off me, and he toppled backward onto the floor laughing. Laurel shot me a look then went back to filling the tub with bubbles from the plastic bottle topped with an elephant head. While I struggled to untangle the tight knots I had put in Malcolm's shoelaces that morning, he lay back on the linoleum, thrilled by his nakedness. His hands found his penis.

"Cut it out, man," I said, pulling off his shoes.

"That's why it's there," Laurel said, reaching under his arms and lifting him up and into the tub.

"Fuck!" I said when the splash wet my shirt and pants.

"That is not helpful," she said. "And it's ugly." Her voice softened as she redirected her attention to Malcolm. "Okay, my love. Want more bubbles?"

I left the bathroom and closed the door behind me. Inside, she struggled to quiet Malcolm, singing "Hush Little Baby."

"Fuck, shit. Fuck, shit. Cock, piss, motherfucker," I whispered, savoring the displeasure on my mother's face when I had sworn a moment earlier, before she'd decided she didn't have the time or energy to care.

I headed out of the trailer and walked toward the beach. I found a fallen palm frond and dragged it down to the water and sat on it. The sea moved listlessly. A few birds lighted on its surface, floated, then took off again like cars at a drive-through. I remembered when I was four or five, a time before Malcolm. I was a skinny kid with arms and legs thin and rubbery as licorice rope. I would plead with Laurel to take me for a swim in "my ocean." The sea was my biggest treasure, a jewel as huge as I could imagine the earth to be, its distant shore my unreachable horizon. Now I imagined myself piloting a boat across the sea, away from this place, away from my mother and brother and the minefield of recrimination that I fumbled across daily. When I was a child making this mental journey, the point was not to reach the other side but to battle the fearsome sea creatures and enormous waves that threatened my tiny skiff. But at twelve, I knew it would take no time at all to get across to Desert Shores or Salton Sea Beach. The journey would be eventless, the destination only a mirror of my town. Those boys from Desert Shores? We played them in basketball. Sometimes they won. Sometimes we did.

I dug my hands through the thin, crusty layer of sand at my feet. I thought about Mrs. Poole and how she must really love her son to keep his high-school picture on her desk where everyone could see it. I hoped I wouldn't get acne. But I thought I probably would since I was a thief and also a trash-talker and there had to be some kind of payback.

When I returned home, Malcolm was already asleep on his couch. Laurel sat at the kitchen table knitting a loose-stitched vest. "He passed out," she said.

"Sorry about the ice cream."

"Maybe sugar isn't such a good idea unless we're really prepared for the consequences."

"You told me that before."

"You probably forgot."

"I didn't forget. I remembered it the whole time."

She looked up from her knitting. "Then why'd you do it?"

"I don't know."

"Were you trying to hurt him?"

I was sure this was the moment: she would say everything right now, accuse me, blame me. My body thrummed with the anticipation of the total obliteration and complete release I would feel when the truth we both labored to hide was finally out in the open. Tears began to form in the corners of my eyes.

"Oh, shoot!" She held her knitting out in front of her, revealing a gaping hole. "I dropped a stitch. Some people know how to fix this kind of mistake . . ." She put the knitting to her face so that her eye lined up with the gap. "I see you," she said, and I knew she could see right into my cruel heart.

FIVE

The next day, I woke to the *boings* and *pops* of a cartoon seeping into my room through the thin walls. Saturdays were Laurel's biggest tip days so I was in charge of Malcolm. It was my job to feed him lunch and sometimes dinner, make sure he didn't get lost in the desert or get fixated on a marble and spend the entire day staring at it. I stayed in bed, hoping he wouldn't require anything for a while, but through a fuzzy half-sleep, I heard the sharp screech of the trailer door opening and the rude snap of it as it closed on its sprung hinge. I considered letting him go on his own at the same time that I envisioned him getting hit by a car on the highway, his body flying up like a rag doll, or drowning, his head sinking quietly below the surface of the water. I knew that all it took for a life to change irreparably was one moment of nonvigilance, one second of letting go.

When I caught up with him, he was already down by the shore. A dry wind scraped across the surface of the water like a ladle peeling off the skin of milk that formed when Laurel made hot chocolate. I squatted behind a thick stand of cholla cactus so that Malcolm wouldn't discover me. I was not in the mood to talk and get nothing in return, and I didn't have the energy for my fantasy games and Malcolm's passive participation. I felt angry with him. Just once, I would have liked him to look at me like he really knew who I was. When we were together, it was all I could do to convince myself that I existed for him at all and that I was not just some innocuous presence like air or heat. I thought about how he must experience life as a smashed mirror, a collection of fractured pieces that never fit together to make a perfect whole. There was this, and that, and the other thing, and all the separate shards didn't really have anything to do with one another, not even the central fact that they were in my brother's brain. How could a person live that way? Most of the ideas that passed through my mind were connected by the idea of *me*. But did he have such self-regard? I tried to imagine thoughts without an identity to organize them, and I was overcome by the knowledge of how easily he could lose himself since he did not take himself into account. How could he survive except by having someone like me or my mother there to assert that he existed at all, even if it was just to say his name? Even if it was just to touch his arm or pretend to know what he wanted?

From my hiding place, I scanned the lake as far as I could see. There were a few terns and maybe a heron—a lean, tilting thing off in the distance—or perhaps it was just the branch of a submerged tree sticking up out of the lake like the arm of a person calling for help. I knew Malcolm was looking for birds, searching for check marks against the unbroken blue sky. Sometimes he would nod his head when he saw birds coming as if he were an air force general silently counting how many airplanes were returning from a mission and how many he had lost. I wondered if Malcolm used words when he counted, or if he had some private language that symbolized amounts to him, or whether, like his thoughts, there was no augmentation, and all he was doing was counting one, and then one, and then one again. Sometimes when I felt agitated, when I wanted to bang hard enough on the wall of the trailer to make a hole and crawl through it, or when I lay in bed on the nights Laurel was out with Richard, fighting my urge to check the lock on the door one more time, I would try counting. But counting never gave me peace the way it did my brother. It only reminded me how enormous the world was, how impossible to grasp, how unbearably limitless.

Malcolm called out to the sky, summoning the birds. His tight fist of a caw traveled across the water. When he heard a noise coming from behind him, his mouth bent into a smile. The birds were coming to him. But the sound was not bird-song, and as he turned, two boys from the neighborhood appeared. I recognized them: Calvin Epps, who sold pills for his older brother Ronald, and Duane Short. They were high school dropouts who trolled the streets of our town with an air of lazy mischief. They howled at Malcolm and tried to imitate him, but they didn't sound like birds at all.

"Shit for brains!"

"Ree-tard!"

My stomach twisted and adrenaline flushed my body, but

for the first time in my life, I made the decision not to do anything. I felt like a different boy, hovering above my old self. I became light-headed, giddy with the notion that this choice to separate myself from my brother was even possible. I listened as the boys continued to taunt Malcolm, and I grew cold inside because I saw the way in which I would one day leave my family, my guilt, and my responsibility behind me. It would not happen by getting in a car or on a bus, or on a boat as I had once thought. It would have to do with my heart hardening just like it was doing now.

Something altered in the air, and the birds appeared. They flew low across the desert just behind the boys, heading toward the water, their long beaks pointing the way, their wings barely moving. They were carried by wind. I wanted to be carried by wind. I wanted to lift off and float on currents of air impossible to see and be taken away from this moment when I was betraying my brother. Malcolm saw the birds. I willed him to say and do nothing, to be normal enough, just this once, to bore these bored boys. But he was oblivious to their taunts, and as he spread his arms on either side of him, he dipped to the right and wheeled around toward the sea. The pelicans touched down on the surface, lowered their beaks, and slapped their wings restlessly against the water. Malcolm jumped up and down and shook his hands. "Awk!" he cried. "Awk-caw!"

The boys laughed and imitated Malcolm, flapping their arms in spastic exaggeration. The ignorant birds fed gracefully. They groomed themselves, their necks wrapping over their backs like casually tossed scarves. Then, as if by agreement, they lifted off and flew away. Malcolm raised his fist in the air and screamed, announcing their departure.

"Fucking freak!"

Malcolm turned toward the boys, his fist still raised, and made his pelican sound again and again. The boys mimicked him, deforming his bird sounds until they were shapeless, ugly noises. Calvin picked up a small rock and threw it, hitting Malcolm in the leg. When Malcolm did not react, Duane picked up a bigger rock and cocked back his arm. Seeing the look of vicious glee on his face woke something powerful in me, a rage that made me stand up and reveal myself. The sound that rumbled through my chest and the hollow tunnel of my throat felt like a tangible thing, a weapon I could use to kill those boys and everything I hated that lived inside me, too. I roared and ran from my hiding place.

I lost the fight almost as soon as it began. Calvin and Duane rushed me, throwing their fists and feet at me until I fell to the ground. I continued to strike out, kicking them, waving my arms above me. When I connected with Calvin's groin, the boys grew more serious about the fight. Their mouths hung open. Spit splattered my face. *Faggot, bastard, cocksucker,* they said, punctuating their words with new assaults. I covered my head with my arms just as a foot landed in my gut. I curled up into a ball.

THE WATER WOKE ME. IT lapped around my feet, soaking my shoes and the bottom half of my pants. I was facedown on the sand. When I rolled over, I felt like a hundred daggers were stabbing me from inside my body. Sand and dirt stuck to my lips and eyelashes. My shirt was ripped, and a bruise below my ribs was already beginning to color. Malcolm lay near me staring peacefully at the sky. The milky foam from the residue of waves lapped around his legs.

"Mal, get out of the water," I said. I stood slowly. The pain was intense, and I bit my lip trying not to cry out. I hobbled over and helped him to his feet. "You're soaking wet, man."

When he took a step, water sloshed inside his canvas sneakers.

"C'mon, Mal," I said, trying not to breathe too deeply because when I did, my chest felt like it would crack open. "We'll go home. We'll dry you off. I'll make us some bacon." I pulled him toward me, but he resisted. He leaned over and tried to brush off his pants but had no luck and only succeeded in coating his palms with sand. He wiped his hands on his T-shirt but it didn't help. I knew what was coming. He started to hum and rock back and forth, holding his hands toward me as if he wanted me to remove them from his body.

"Okay," I said. "No problem." I crouched down, bringing him with me, and placed his hands in the sea. The dirt fell away from his skin, swirling into the water in lazy spirals. I washed his hands until they were clean. "You're okay now," I said.

Suddenly I was so tired and sore I could not imagine walking back to the trailer, wrestling him into dry clothes, making food. I moved up the beach, sat on a rusted hubcap, and watched the water nudge the shore, depositing something dark on the sand. Malcolm grabbed the object.

"Mom's not going to let you keep any more crap, man," I said as he walked toward me with his treasure, although I knew I was wrong. She would praise this piece of garbage like she praised all his finds, as if he had discovered gold. "That's cool, though," I said. "Let me see." I took it in my hand, cried out, and dropped it onto the ground. I heard myself say, "Oh, shit, oh, shit!" and "Fuck, Malcolm. What the fuck?" It was a gun.

Malcolm bent down to take his prize, but I pushed him away. "Don't touch it." I said. "Don't. Just—" I picked up the gun, ran to the shoreline, and hurled it back to the sea.

Malcolm screamed. "Ma, ma, ma!" He ran to the water.

I grabbed him by the waist and held him back. "It's gone now," I said, struggling to keep hold of him as he writhed in my arms. "It's bye-bye." But I had not thrown the gun far enough, and it came back again like a faithful dog. "You can't have it, Mal," I said. "It's bad. I'll find you something good. A rock, maybe. I'll get Mom to let you keep it."

He jabbed his elbow into one of my bruises and I screamed and let go of him. He ran to the shore, but I recovered and pushed in front of him. Splashing through the water, I picked up the gun. I ran up the beach and hurled it into the brush.

"It's gone," I said when Malcolm caught up to me. "It was never here." He made a strangled sound of frustration. "You'll forget about it," I said, hoping the gun would be like the stick guns, and bullet casings, and all the things that passed through his mind like vagrants, finding no reason to abide in such a fruitless place. I found a piece of driftwood among the shrubs and handed it to Malcolm. "This is a good one. This is special."

I pointed it into the air and made the firing sound of a gun. "Here," I said. "We'll play bank robbers, okay? You be my lookout. You shoot anybody who comes near."

Still moaning, he took the wood and threw it. It sailed through the air end over end. He ran to retrieve it, cradled it in his arms, and raced for home.

WHEN LAUREL RETURNED FROM WORK, part of me wanted to strip off my shirt and show her the red and purple colored galaxies that covered my torso, to blame her for not being there that day to protect us. But I hid my wounds. I could imagine her taking the matter into her own hands, striding over to Calvin's trailer and berating him, setting me up for even more trouble. After dinner, she washed Malcolm's hair. When they were finished, she led him out of the bathroom, dressed him, then sat on a chair, pulling him onto her lap. She dragged a comb through his slick black locks. Malcolm tilted his head back as she drew the comb down. His smile revealed the rose-colored flesh inside of his mouth.

"I'm going out," I said.

"Where?"

"To ride my bike."

"It's going to get dark soon. Take a flashlight."

As I went to get the flashlight from the kitchen drawer, she stopped combing Malcolm's hair and studied me. "You know what I do when you're not home?" she said.

"No."

"I wait for you to get back."

"You just sit here?"

"No. But everything I do? In my mind, I'm doing it while I'm waiting for you to come home. I say, 'I'll bake these cookies while I wait for Ares' or 'I'll clip my toenails while I wait for Ares.' "

"You're obsessed with toenails."

"If I didn't clip yours, they'd be claws by now."

"I can clip my own nails."

"Come here," she said, holding her arms out. Malcolm slid off her lap.

She waited for me, but I couldn't make my body move to her as it had done hundreds of times before. "I'm just going to ride my bike, Mom. Don't make such a big deal about everything."

Malcolm ran to me.

"No, man," I said. "Not this time."

"Take him."

"Come on, Mom."

"He wants to go with you."

"Jesus! Can't I ever do anything by myself?"

"Excuse me?"

"I just want to go for a ride."

"And I just want someone to give me a million dollars. But that's not going to happen. At least not tonight." She smiled at me, and I knew I had lost.

WHEN WE REACHED THE SEA, we dropped our bikes in the dirt. I led Malcolm to the shore, hoping that he would become distracted by something there and not notice what I was doing, but he was captivated by the flashlight beam and returned to where I was training it on the creosote and sage. The beam moved across fast food wrappers and cigarette butts, tufts of desert grass and shattered pieces of concrete, then landed on a piece of rotting plywood on top of which sat the gun. It looked more real than it did when Malcolm rescued it from the sea, and I was fascinated by its sleek squared-off shape and by the notion that such a small thing could stop a life. In all my imaginings of war, I had never thought I would ever handle an actual weapon. The moment I held it I knew the power and sense of safety it bestowed on me would be hard to give up. I had heard stories of soldiers who named their guns and treated them like favored pets, and I understood why. I was now a boy who had a gun. It would be impossible to return to being the weak and helpless boy I had been.

I could not keep the gun at home or even near my home. Malcolm was too adept a discoverer of the castoff and hidden. So we rode our bikes beyond town, over the rugged access road that hugged the shore, stopping when I felt sure we had traveled so far that even if Malcolm were to set out in this direction thinking he remembered something, he would forget his purpose along the way. We dropped our bikes near a Department of Public Works sign and followed a drainage ditch that led down to the water. I chose a random spot and began to dig with my hands. It was difficult to make a dent in the sun-hardened topsoil until I found a rock and used it to break the ground. Malcolm kneeled next to me and started to paw the earth, and even though I yelled at him and told him to go away, he continued. As we worked, I worried that I might not be able to dig deep enough to make a proper hiding place for my treasure. Because the gun was *my* treasure, and I wanted to keep it safe in a place only I would know about.

Malcolm lost interest in digging, and after I cleaned his hands, he wandered off to inspect the broken fencing along the access road. When the hole was deep enough, I took the gun from my pocket and dropped it in. The sound of a car rose up in the distance. Quickly, I shoveled dirt back into the hole. I found some stones and placed them on top, but then reconsidered. The mound of rocks looked like a grave or one of the roadside markers people built to commemorate the spot where someone was killed in a car accident so I left the place bare of anything that would call attention to itself. Instead, I memorized the pattern of nearby bushes, which seemed to form an L ending at my gun's grave. As Malcolm and I rode back home, I prayed for a night wind to kick up and blow a new layer of dirt over the bike tracks and our footprints, at the same time reassuring myself that no one would come to that spot because the only reason to go there was to get high or have sex, and people who did those things weren't looking to expose anything. They had secrets, too.

SIX

Malcolm was in trouble. I could tell by the look on the school secretary's face when she came into social studies and by the way she conferred with my teacher instead of simply calling my name and asking me to come, that Malcolm had done something far worse than escape his classroom. As we walked down the hall, I heard noises coming from room 23 that sounded like kids trying to imitate ghosts. Inside the room all was chaos. Malcolm cowered under a desk. A girl named Maria Elena screamed and pulled her hair. A puddle of urine on the floor sent up a sharp stench. Mrs. Murphy tried to calm Maria Elena, holding the girl's arms away from her face, which bore an angry, bleeding scratch. I crawled under the desk where Malcolm was rocking back and forth, cradling a dead bird in his hands.

The school secretary had taken over trying to help Maria Elena, while Mrs. Murphy crouched down next to Malcolm and me. When Malcolm saw her, he screamed and hid the bird from her.

"Maria Elena brought it in for show and tell," Mrs.

Murphy said, her voice shaking. "It was her bird and it died last night. She wanted to share."

There were traces of blood on Malcolm's fingers. The secretary was placing a Band-Aid on Maria Elena's cheek.

"We cannot have him attacking other children," Mrs. Murphy said.

"Okay, man," I said to Malcolm, ignoring her. "It's okay."

"It is not okay. He has to give back the bird," she said. "It doesn't belong to him."

"It's okay," I repeated, holding him and rocking with him.

"Give me the bird, Malcolm," she said.

"Wait a minute," I said.

"Give the bird to me now!"

"Wait a minute!"

She gave me a sharp look and stood up. She stayed by the table, her legs inches from my face. I wanted to reach out and rip a hole in her stockings, make her go away. "Shhh," I whispered into Malcolm's hair. "Shhh . . ." Finally he calmed, but I couldn't convince him to give up the bird. Maria Elena began to cry louder. Mrs. Murphy crouched back down. "We need this to be over, do you understand?" she hissed. "The other children are disturbed."

"He thinks she killed the bird," I said.

"She didn't kill the bird. It died. Birds die."

"That's not what he thinks."

She exhaled heavily. "I don't really know what he thinks." She reached out and tried to force the bird from him. He lunged toward her and she shrieked, pulling back her hand.

Two pearls of blood began to form on her skin where Malcolm's teeth marks were visible. She slapped him across the face.

MALCOLM AND I SAT OUTSIDE the principal's office waiting for Laurel. Occasionally the school secretary glanced up, and I could feel her judgment. I wanted to tell her and the principal and all the people who looked at my brother with curiosity and pity that although Malcolm might have done something wrong, he was not capable of intention and so couldn't be punished. But I knew those were my mother's thoughts trying to drum out what I had seen: Malcolm had known what he was doing when he bit Mrs. Murphy and he probably knew what he was doing when he scratched Maria Elena. He attacked the people he thought were hurting the bird. Laurel would never admit it, but I had seen volition in his eyes. I tried to chase away those thoughts, tried to hear Laurel telling me that everyone else was wrong and we were right, that Malcolm was perfect and innocent and special, but these excuses felt empty.

Finally I heard the suck of rubber sandals on the slick hallway floor outside the office, and I knew my mother had come. Her work shoes had octopus-like cups on the bottom of the soles that I used to play with, walking them along the sides of the tub while I bathed, pretending to be Jacques Cousteau. She appeared in the office door, along with the sweet tang of eucalyptus oil, wearing her uniform with "Serenity Spa" written in cursive over one breast. Her face was flushed as if she had run all the way from Palm Springs to school. When she knelt in front of Malcolm, I saw the blue patch of her underwear between her legs. I glanced at the secretary, hoping she couldn't see. Laurel's heedless exposure made her seem vulnerable and pathetic. My heart sank. She took Malcolm's hands in hers. "Mommy's here. Mommy's here," she murmured softly. Malcolm inhaled a laugh.

Mr. Philipson opened the door to the principal's office. He wore tan slacks, a short-sleeved shirt, and heavy glasses that were pushed up onto his forehead as if he had eyes there. "Mrs. Connors?"

Laurel stood abruptly, patting down her dress, adjusting her purse over her shoulder. "Ms.," she said. "There's no mister."

Philipson didn't respond, only opened his door wider and gestured for her to come in.

"Come on, boys," she said to us.

"I think it would be better if we talked alone," he said.

"We don't have secrets in our family."

"Still, I think it would be better." He placed his hand lightly on the small of her back, guiding her into his office. To my surprise, she didn't put up a fight. Twenty minutes later, when she reappeared, she looked shrunken. She held her purse to her chest.

"You can go back to class now, Ares," Philipson said.

"I'm taking my boys home," she said quietly.

"There are still two periods left in the day, Ms. Connors."

"I'm taking my boys home," she repeated, her voice shaking.

I knew I should have felt happy to be missing math and PE. Since my mother did not stop to let me get my books from my locker, I would not have to do homework that night. But I wanted to stay. For the first time, I wanted to be separate from my mother and my brother. As we walked through the disconcertingly empty halls of the school, the muffled sounds of teachers' voices seeped out from under closed doors, and I felt left out of something I desperately wanted to be included in. I tried to remember the area of a circle, or how to divide with decimals, or the definition of the Monroe Doctrine. I remembered all those things perfectly and wished dearly that I could go to class and tell my teachers what I knew. I wanted to be like all the other kids who didn't have brothers who bit people and put things in piles, who had mothers who cared if their underwear showed. Resentment blossomed into hatred. I hated the back of Laurel's knees with their horizontal red creases and protruding blue veins. I despised the snap of her sandals on the pavement as we walked toward our car. But my hatred turned inward because I knew that in five minutes, or an hour, or a day, I would need her, maybe more fiercely for all my terrible thoughts about her, and I despised myself for this.

Her silence on the way home was like a warning, and I knew I shouldn't ask any questions like what were we supposed to do now that Malcolm had bit a teacher, now that we could not protect him, imagine what he wanted and give it to him, make all the adjustments that would ensure the fantasy that he was normal and everyone who didn't think so was strange. Once home, Laurel announced that her back hurt. She went into her room, closed the card curtain, and lay down on her bed. I played with Malcolm, building igloos out of pillows. I tried to spin a polar explorer fantasy, designating him as my Eskimo guide, but I didn't have the heart to assume his silent involvement and I dropped the game before we harpooned our first whale with a broom handle. We watched TV for the rest of the afternoon. Laurel didn't even come out of her room to assert her hour-a-day rule, but this little victory meant nothing to me.

Finally, at dinnertime, she emerged from her room. Her face was red and puffy from crying. She reheated the vegetable soup she had made the night before, and we ate it with saltine crackers. She didn't touch her soup, but rested her chin on her hands and looked intently at Malcolm as he broke his crackers into halves, then quarters, then lined the pieces up.

"Maybe he wants to count," I said.

"Oh, I don't know," she said wearily, and I was frightened by her unwillingness to invent his purpose. "Apparently I'm not doing the right things for him," she said. "Apparently he needs to be tested or else they will not keep him in special ed. Apparently I have to fill out forms."

"They want to kick him out of school?"

"Mrs. Murphy required stitches. And he hurt that girl."

"It was only a scratch."

"I've always known who my boys are," she said, ignoring me. "No one can tell me they know my boys better than I do." But her voice was fragile, as if she no longer believed herself.

While she went outside to empty the garbage and talk to Mrs. Vega next door, I took a half-eaten pack of M&M's I'd bought a week earlier and waved it in front of Malcolm's face. He reached for the candy, but I pulled it back. Then I ran around the room drawing a fly's inscrutable pattern with my body and hid the candy beneath the sofa cushion. Malcolm searched frantically while I watched, hoping that frustration and desire would compel words out of his mouth. "Warm," I coaxed him. "Warmer. No, getting colder. No, Mal, you're freezing now." I moved a step closer to the couch, trying to draw him toward it, but I could tell he was losing focus and that he was beginning to forget what he was looking for. I reached beneath the cushion and grabbed the candy. "Mal," I said, desperately trying to win back his disloyal mind. "Look, Mal. Look what I have."

"Stop it!" Laurel had come inside without my hearing her. She stepped toward me, snatched the candy from my hand and gave it to Malcolm. "Here, baby," she said. "Here's what you're looking for." Then she turned to me. Her face registered not anger but hurt, as if she'd caught me torturing a cat and couldn't imagine a world in which a child could be capable of such cruelty. "Why did you do that?" Her eyes glittered. "Why do you tease him like that?"

"I just thought . . ." I drifted off, bereft of any rational answer.

"Thought what? That it's fun to fool your six-year-old brother? Are you like all those other kids?"

"No!"

"Then what?"

"I thought it would help."

"Help?"

"If he talks, maybe they'll let him back in school."

She was silent.

"Come here," she said finally. She took a step toward me, and I recoiled. She put her hands on my shoulders. The gentleness of her touch made me shrivel up inside. She pulled me to her and whispered into my ear. "We have to stick together, the three of us," she said. "Everyone else has an agenda. What's good for *them*. What makes it easier for *them* . . ." Her voice trailed off. She smelled of the complicated creams she used at work. I held my breath but I couldn't avoid the eucalyptus and rosewater and something plastic and slightly medicinal, and beneath those odors her warm, yeasty smell. I fought my urge to melt into that familiarity. I shrugged away from her grip.

She stared at me, and then tears spilled down her cheeks. Sitting down on a chair, she reached out and pulled Malcolm onto her lap. She stroked the place on the top of his head where he had fallen so many years ago, her finger circling the spot. My chest tightened as I waited for her accusation. He leaned his head against her chest, smiling with pleasure at her attentions. "Why isn't what he is good enough?" she said quietly. "Isn't it good enough?" She looked at me, her eyes wide and searching, as if I had the answer.

Later she gave him a bath. I lay on my bed, listening to the water hitting the floor of the bathroom and Malcolm's high, atonal song echo off the tub. I thought about the mop, which leaned upside down against the outside of the trailer, its hair stiff and matted, and about the frayed towels stored underneath Laurel's bed. I knew it would take a lot of work to sop up the flood Malcolm was making, and that it would be up to me to do the job. And I knew that I would do it because my rebellion was still a stranger to me, something I had not come to trust completely and so I would fall back on my old habits. I got up and stood in the open door of the bathroom. Laurel knelt by the side of the tub. Malcolm's face was layered with a meringue of bubbles, and soapy water covered the floor. She had laid a towel down to kneel on, but it was drenched as was the hem of her pink uniform. She used tweezers to dig the remnants of Maria Elena's blood out from under Malcolm's fingernails. When she was done, she watched him splash and play. His mouth cracked open into a wide, frothy grin, and her face gave way to a soft smile.

"Look at him," she said. "There's no violence in that child." She stood, kicked off her sandals, and climbed into the tub. A dark stain crept up the material of her dress all the way to her chest. She sat back and let out a delighted yelp as water rose to her chin. She turned to me, as happy as I'd ever seen her. "Come on in, baby," she said. "The water's just fine."

THE FOLLOWING MONDAY BEFORE CLASSES began, I took Malcolm to the library. Mrs. Poole had set up a kid-sized desk in the corner with small chairs on either side.

SEVEN

The following week after school let out, Malcolm and I rode our bikes to Mrs. Poole's house. Philipson had told my mother that if Malcolm attended once-a-week sessions with the librarian, and if his behavior improved in the classroom, he would be allowed to stay in school. Mrs. Poole lived in a part of Niland that had houses and lawns. Her low, ranch-style home was freshly painted an egg-yolk yellow that stood out among the other drab and sun-faded exteriors on her street. The front door was made of wood and beveled glass, which revealed a ghostly shadow as she came from within her house and opened it. I followed Malcolm inside, but she stopped me.

"You can do your homework on the porch," she said. "We need quiet."

While they worked in the kitchen, I sat outside, trying to concentrate on my studies, but I was distracted by the unfamiliar surroundings. At one point, I looked through the window. Mrs. Poole sat close to Malcolm at the table, never taking her eyes off him while she talked and made big gestures and held up flash cards and different-shaped blocks. I couldn't hear what she was saying but I could tell by watching her mouth that she spoke slowly, as if she thought Malcolm's problem was that he was a foreigner who didn't understand English.

I walked around the perimeter of the house. Mrs. Poole had laid out a substantial garden on one side. There were tomato plants bending under the weight of large ripening fruits. A strange kind of lettuce spread out in a fan, its leaves scalloped in lazy curves. Oblong yellow squash lay on top of the dirt like fat baseball bats. We did not eat foods like squash or exotic lettuces at home, and the only gardens I'd ever seen were studded with cactus and other drought-resistant plants that seemed untended. In Mrs. Poole's backyard, a white wrought iron table and three matching chairs sat in the middle of the grass, which was wet and spongy due to all the watering it must have taken to keep it green. A short distance away at the fence line stood a white gazebo. A single chair, the fourth of the wrought iron set, sat inside the structure as if it were taking some time alone to think. I tried to picture Mrs. Poole sitting in that chair. Maybe she read library books there. Or maybe she went there when she wanted to think about her son. Mrs. Poole's house was not large but it wasn't a trailer, and the way it spoke so simply of a life different from the one I knew filled me with awe.

At the end of the hour, she and Malcolm appeared at the front door. "Tell your mother he did very well," she told me. "And I'll see him next week at the same time."

"Okay."

"How was the tour?"

"What?"

"I saw you walking around the house."

My face grew hot.

"It's a good idea to ask for permission before you wander around another person's property. Some people might not like being snooped on."

"I wasn't snooping."

"Different families have different rules, Ares. It's important to remember that."

All the way home, I replayed her chastisement, feeling freshly humiliated with each passing mile. But by the time we arrived at the trailer, I realized I was holding on to the moment because like a good dream or a heroic fantasy, I did not want to let it and Mrs. Poole go. It felt oddly gratifying to be the object of her precise censure; I had strayed and been contained, and beneath my embarrassment I felt a relief I had never experienced. No matter how much I might try to please my mother, I knew that I never really could because I had done something so terrible to my brother that her love could only be qualified. But I could please Mrs. Poole just by following her rules. I could be a boy who was not shadowed by an old, mongrel guilt. At her house, I could reinvent myself as a boy who did things right.

"MRS. POOLE SAID HE DID a good job," I announced proudly when Laurel came home from work late that afternoon.

"Is that what she said?" she sighed, exhausted. She

stepped out of her sandals and unbuttoned her uniform as she walked into her room.

"I think he had fun," I said, deflated by her lack of enthusiasm for my report.

"How do you know?" She drew her uniform over her head. I saw her purple bra and her beige panties and the subtle torque of her backbone as she bent to loosen her muscles there.

"He laughed," I said. "A bunch of times."

She pulled on shorts and a tank top. "Well that's good," she said, without much conviction. "I guess laughing is good." She came into the main room and sat down on the chair opposite the couch, her legs splayed. "I'm wrecked," she said, massaging one hand with the other. "Retirement makes a lot of people very tense." She let her head fall over the chair as though she were taking in the sun. "So, what did that lady make him do?"

"I don't know. I'm not allowed inside."

"What do you mean?" she said, bringing her head forward.

"She said it's distracting for Mal."

"She better not be doing anything weird in there."

"She's not! They sit at a table. He plays with blocks. She gives him snacks."

She studied me as if searching out a lie. "Well, I suppose she knows what she's doing. They have me up against a wall, those school people." She looked over at Malcolm, who was watching television with the sound turned off. Her eyes softened. "You have to tell me if it upsets him to go there, okay, Ares?" she said. "You have to be my eyes and ears."

"I will."

"Because I'll yank him right out of there if she's making him feel bad, or sad, or scared. I will. I don't care if they never let him back into that school again."

I wanted to defend Mrs. Poole because Laurel knew nothing about her son, or what the other kids at school said about him, or about the pleasure I felt being in the librarian's precise and orderly universe. But I decided Mrs. Poole was a secret I would keep to myself. She would serve as the boundary between my mother and me that I craved but hadn't figured out how to draw. I would not tell Laurel about the vegetables that Mrs. Poole was able to grow in her garden, or about her gazebo, or about her smile that, when offered, was like a present. "Mrs. Poole is nice," I said.

"My parents were 'nice,' " she said. "They could win the award for nice. That lady is just one more obstacle." She stood and opened the refrigerator, staring into it as if waiting for it to speak to her. "You have to be careful," she said. "You don't want to end up on the wrong side."

"Of what?"

She shut the refrigerator door without taking out any food or answering me.

RICHARD ARRIVED AN HOUR LATER for dinner. Malcolm was more than usually excited by the food. Laurel always buried a hard-boiled egg in the middle of her meatloaf, and he watched as Richard ceremoniously carved. With each falling slice, Malcolm bounced in his seat, waiting for the first glimpse of the slick, off-colored egg.

"He remembers!" Laurel said happily.

That he remembered the location of this particular treasure from week to week made my stomach turn. I thought about the gun and hoped he would not remember where it lay buried.

"Hmmm," Richard said, peering down at the meat through his round glasses. "Maybe she forgot this time." He grinned, but Laurel frowned and shook her head.

"Kids don't get sarcasm," she said, laying a protective hand on Malcolm's arm.

"Kids get everything," Richard said, winking at me. He carved another impossibly thin slice.

"You're driving him crazy," Laurel said happily. "You're driving me crazy."

"It's good to know I can drive you crazy."

Malcolm erupted with a high-pitched squeal when he spied the first hint of egg peeking out from the grey-brown of the meat.

"Ahh," Laurel said. She squeezed Richard's shoulder, leaned over, and kissed him. The kiss turned long and deep. An image of my mother and Richard having sex appeared in my mind. They looked like one of the pictures in her *Kama Sutra* book—Richard on his knees, his huge penis pointing at her like a warning finger. I tried to erase the image by focusing on the meatloaf, but the egg made me feel ill, its arrival reminding me of some perversion of a birth scene. I wondered if anyone had been around to exclaim over my arrival. It had never occurred to me to ask. I knew Laurel had delivered me at home, but I had never wondered who was there with her and had always imagined that somehow she had managed the whole thing on her own, delivering me on the trailer floor in her self-sufficient way, getting up after it was all over to make herself a cup of ginger tea. When she was pregnant with Malcolm, a doctor told her that the baby was too small and that she had better give birth under medical care in case something went wrong. Late one night, she woke me and drove us to the hospital, every so often pulling to the side of the road until a contraction eased. During her labor, she told me I shouldn't worry if the baby was covered in blood because it wasn't hurt, and that I shouldn't be worried if she made funny noises or screamed in pain because it was not the kind of pain that made a person sad but the kind that made them the happiest they'd ever been. I could not imagine pain that made a person happy. Hours into the labor, she shrieked so fiercely I thought she was dying, and I flung myself across her body. A nurse pulled me away and, despite Laurel's protests, told me to leave the room. Relieved, I sat on the floor of the corridor and studied the shoes and rolling wheels that hurried past, trying to ignore the sounds coming from the delivery room. At one point the door opened and a nurse walked out, and I heard someone say, "Does the father want to be present?" and someone else said, "No father on the chart."

Before Richard sliced the rest of the loaf, Laurel fished out the entire egg with a spoon and put it on Malcolm's plate, where it spun lazily. Malcolm picked it up and rolled it in his hands. He would not eat it. He would admire it, rub it against his cheek, and then he would put it on his shelf of treasures and trash where Laurel would allow it to remain until it started to smell. Richard dropped a slice of meatloaf onto each plate. He reached for the ketchup and poured a steady stream over his food.

"Maybe next time I should skip the meat and just serve ketchup for dinner," Laurel said.

"Army," Richard said, by way of explanation. Once he told me that when he couldn't sleep he patrolled outside his trailer, listening for the sounds of life in the desert brush. He claimed he could distinguish a human sound from that of an animal, that he could even tell the sound of a man from a woman.

A helicopter flew over the house so low I ducked my head. A shaft from the copter's spotlight flared in the windows. "Something's going on," Laurel said, not looking up from her meal. Malcolm was distracted by the light and craned his neck around the room, following its trajectory.

"They're flying a little far off base tonight," Richard said. "Unless it's a drug bust."

"Okay, baby," Laurel said, gently turning Malcolm's head back toward his meal. "Let's do one thing at a time."

The light lingered around the perimeter of the trailer before it and the sound of the helicopter faded away. I stared at my plate, my heart pounding. I was certain they had found the gun. They would find my fingerprints, and I would be accused of stealing it. Maybe I would be put in the same prison as Mrs. Poole's son. I wondered if prisoners wore pajamas or if they just slept in their prison clothes. The helicopter returned, the beam lighting us briefly as it swept past.

"Sounds like a Huey," Richard said. "That *k-ching,*

k-ching." The multicolored lights from a passing police car danced across our wall.

Malcolm stood and began to spin around the room with his arms on either side of him like airplane wings. "Awm! Awm!" he cried.

"So much for dinner," Laurel said, putting down her fork. She stood and reached for Malcolm and began to dance with him. He hugged her and leaned his head back so that his face was nearly upside down. "You're going to barf up all that good food," she said, gently slowing him to a stop. "Alright, buddy. Let's go see what all the fuss is about. Let's go, Ares."

"I'm not done eating," I said. I thought I should run away. I wondered how long it would take me to bike over the border to Mexicali.

"You can stay if you want," she said. "I want to see what's going on."

Richard took a pocketknife from his jeans and extracted the toothpick. "Is this the evening's entertainment?" he asked, rolling the bone-colored pick back and forth across his lips with his tongue.

"At least it's free," Laurel said, leading Malcolm out the door.

Richard looked across the table at me. There was something about his watchfulness that made me think he was onto me and my secrets. "Do you like to watch car accidents?" he said.

"I don't know."

"Most people do. Most people will slow down on the road to see what happened. You know why?"

I looked down at my plate.

"People like to see terrible things happen to other people."

"Okay," I said uncomfortably.

"But what people don't get is that the terrible thing is happening to *them*. When they speed back up and turn on their radio and forget about what they just saw. That's the terrible thing. We're all implicated."

I could not meet his eyes.

"Come on, kiddo," he said finally, his chair stuttering along the floor as he stood up. "Let's go see the show."

Crowds had gathered at the shore. I recognized most people: Ed, who owned the general store, his wife, Vera. The kid who played varsity football and was supposed to get recruited by San Diego State was standing next to Calvin's brother Ronald, the dealer. Ronald wore the beat-up leather jacket I always saw him in, no matter how hot the day. Mrs. Vega, wearing a flowered apron over her caftan, stood with her son Milo, who was grown but still lived at home. It seemed that the few hundred inhabitants of Bombay Beach had dropped whatever they were doing and come from their homes, cocking their heads curiously as if emerging from hibernation. Down by the water's edge Richard stood behind Laurel, his fingers caught in the belt loops of her shorts. A Coast Guard boat sat on the water, lit up like a power plant. The helicopter circled, its cone of light tracing a wobbly figure eight on the sea. The sound obliterated all conversation. I saw the bodies of divers appear and disappear beneath the surface like the dark, slick backs of dolphins.

"What do you think?" Laurel yelled above the noise.

"I think they're using a lot of your tax money to get whatever is under there out of there," Richard said.

The divers surfaced holding something between them. Others on the deck of the boat hauled the object on board.

"Oh my God," Laurel said. "Is that a body?"

"Two arms, two legs," Richard said.

I thought I would throw up. I reminded myself that I had not killed anyone. I had only found and buried a gun. I looked over at Malcolm, wondering what he remembered. Maybe nothing, maybe all of it. The helicopter veered away from the scene. I watched the cone of light slide across the water, grow faint, then disappear as the helicopter rose higher in the sky.

"Dead people in the water. This is a crazy-ass place," Richard sighed, shaking his head dolefully.

"You come back year after year," Laurel said.

"I come back for you."

"You're a liar," she said, smiling.

"Your mother's a real romantic," he said to me, wrapping his arms around her shoulders.

"I'm a realist," she said.

"That's no fun."

"Have you ever noticed," she said, staring out across the dark water, "that whatever you fantasize about never actually happens? You just end up disappointed."

"Maybe you have the wrong fantasies," he said. "Life isn't like on TV, right, Ares? Nobody finds a free car behind door number one." He looked at me closely. "What's wrong with you, boy? Looks like you saw a ghost."

Laurel put an arm around my shoulder. "Did that scare you, baby?"

"No," I said, shrugging out of her hold.

The motor of the boat erupted as it headed away from the shore. The crowd broke up, and people began to drift back toward their homes. Someone popped open a beer can. Some kids laughed. Their sound jangled in the night like a few loose coins in a pocket.

"Well, I'm freaked out," Laurel said, taking Malcolm by the hand and moving away from the sea. "Let's go home, baby."

I looked back toward the water one more time. The sky was not quite black. I could make out bands of low clouds hanging like laundry lines. By the shore, I thought I saw a firefly draw its erratic design in the dark. But the spark was just the lit end of Richard's cigarette. He stood alone by the water's edge. After a moment, he released a sigh of pale smoke.

LAUREL WAS UNNERVED BY THE dead body, so for the first time ever Richard spent the night at our house. I slept in my mother's bed so she and Richard could have the privacy of my room. I lay awake listening to their groans and sniffles, the low murmur of their conversation, my narrow bed complaining under the weight of two adult bodies. I got up and walked through the card curtain, careful not to make noise and startle Malcolm into one of his terrors as I headed out the trailer door. The night air was cool, and I sat down on the metal steps, hunching over my knees to keep warm. The leaves of Laurel's struggling plants tickled my arms. I thought about the dead body in the sea, how it was forever separated from the life that once inhabited it. In science class, we had cut a worm in half and watched as each part continued to squirm inside the petri dish, a headless body, a bodiless head. Students screamed with delight. Some boys pretended to vomit. A girl cried. The disturbing image of the severed body stayed with me for weeks after the experiment. The worm, not realizing that its life was over, thought that it could somehow continue to live despite the impossible fact of its situation. I felt sorry for the worm not because I had killed it with a razor blade, but because the two halves seemed so witless, each searching for a futile purpose.

I must have fallen asleep sitting up because I was woken when the front door of the trailer opened against my back, pushing me off the steps and onto the ground.

"Sorry, man. Didn't know you were camping out," Richard said, helping me up. He dusted off my back like I was a jacket he meant to put on. Craning his neck to see the starry sky, he drew in a long, deep breath. "Not a bad idea, camping out. Your mother's kind of sleep is impossible to sleep next to. It's like lying beside a corpse."

"So I don't get my room back tonight?"

"Tough not having privacy at your age."

"You too," I said, thinking of the sounds I'd heard them making.

A slow smile crossed his face. "You don't miss a trick," he said. "C'mon. We'll get her out of there."

"It's okay. I don't mind."

"No. A boy should have his space."

Reluctantly, I followed him back inside. The door to my bedroom stood open, and I saw my mother asleep on my bed, her form outlined by the sheet. One pale leg was exposed and in the spill from the outdoor floods it looked like marble. Richard slid his hands underneath her shoulders and knees and started to lift her. "Get the sheet," he whispered. But before I could, the sheet slid halfway off her revealing a breast and the hair at her crotch. I froze, not because I had never seen her body but because Richard was there, and my mother was unconscious, and everything felt illicit in a way it never had before. I didn't want to touch her. She murmured something in her sleep and turned her head toward Richard's chest.

"Can I have some help here?" he hissed, irritable under the strain of her weight.

Trying not to touch her skin, I adjusted the sheet and stood back while he carried her out the door. His movements were precise and stealthy. I wondered whether this was what war was like: carrying out missions in the jungle in the middle of the night, communicating only through sharp whispers and swift gestures, making sure not to do anything random that might increase the likelihood of being seen and killed. The ease with which he moved made me think he must have carried a lot of bodies away from further harm and that he must have been very calm around dead people.

In the living room he motioned for me to pull back the card curtain. He passed through and laid Laurel on her bed.

When he covered her with unexpected gentleness, I understood for the first time that the feelings that traveled between my mother and Richard had nothing to do with me. I felt betrayed, not by them but by my younger self who had naively accepted everything and had not looked beyond the near horizon of my life to see how insignificant I was. Richard brushed hair off her face. He let his hand linger on her cheek then removed it swiftly like he was pulling a pick-up stick out of a pile, trying to trick the other sticks into not recognizing their loss.

"*Sayonara*, kiddo," he whispered, signaling good-bye with an ironic salute as he left the trailer, closing the door gently behind him. When I heard the engine of his Jeep start I turned the lock on the door, listening for the sound of its secure, final snap.

Neighborhood gossip was finally confirmed by an article in the local newspaper a few days later, which reported that a Mexican farmworker had been found drowned in the sea. There was no report of a missing gun and no indication that the man had been shot. There was speculation that he had killed himself but this was unconfirmed. My mother and the others in our neighborhood shook their heads at the news, let it linger in their minds and on their lips for a few days. But after a short while, the death of that stranger became just another one of the unquestioned comings and goings that we took as part of the natural history of our desert home.

EIGHT

At Malcolm's third session a light and unexpected rain was falling, so Mrs. Poole allowed me inside her house. She told me that I could do my homework in the living room but that I was not to turn on the television because there was no door separating the living room from the kitchen.

"You can sit there," she said, motioning me toward a low cushioned chair next to a shelf full of books. "Use the lamp. You don't want to hurt your eyes." She watched me while I took my seat as if she didn't trust me to follow her directions. As I turned on the lamp, I worried that I'd already made a mistake and would be banished again, but she smiled and returned to the kitchen without saying anything further.

The material on my chair was a rough orange plaid that matched the material of the couch. Brass rivets connected the cushions to the chair, which made me imagine castles and thrones. From where I sat, I studied the room. Rough bricks surrounded the fireplace. Four of them stood out from the wall, and small porcelain figurines perched on them like people deciding whether or not to jump. A set of shiny brass fireplace pokers and brooms stood next to the fire screen. The miniature tools appealed to me and I wanted to hold them, swing them around like swords, and pretend I *was* in a castle and these were my weapons. But I knew that if I moved them Mrs. Poole would find out. There was something about the order of the room that was undeniably deliberate. I could feel her hand on each object, placing it just so. The window shades were drawn against the harsh sun, and the twilit room felt as if a spell had been cast on it.

Every so often I heard Mrs. Poole and Malcolm, their voices rising above the low buzz of the house's electricity like the apexes of waves. Carefully, I laid my books on the burled shag carpeting and inspected the photographs on the shelves. There were many framed pictures of Mrs. Poole and a man I guessed to be her husband. He wore a beard and mustache and black, square-framed glasses. In one picture he wore the khaki uniform of a state trooper. Being in the presence of a policeman, even just the photograph of one, made me acutely aware that I was disobeying Mrs. Poole and that I should be doing my homework. In the kitchen, she was still chanting to Malcolm in her firm, insistent voice: "*Book, bah, bah, book . . . Can you say that?*"

Farther along the mantle sat framed shots of Mr. and Mrs. Poole standing with Kevin. In one, he was younger than in the photo on Mrs. Poole's library desk—he might have been my age. He didn't have pimples, and his face was fuller and softer. He stood in front of the Pooles' house, a red, child-sized suitcase at his feet. In another, he was older, standing astride a dirt bike, while Mrs. Poole stood to his left, looking at him as if he were a curious stranger.

A chair scraped against the kitchen floor. I hurried back to my designated seat, picked up my notebook, and pretended to work, but Mrs. Poole did not come into the living room after all, and my eyes wandered to the coffee table. Mrs. Poole subscribed to *Ladies' Home Journal* and *Cosmopolitan* and a TV fan magazine, which I picked up. I turned to an article about Charlene Tilton. The picture showed her posing in a tight dress, and the outline of her nipples showed beneath the thin material. Malcolm let out a shout, and I dropped the magazine back onto the pile. Remembering my mother's instructions, I went to the kitchen doorway to see if he was upset. His back was to me. Mrs. Poole held up her hand to stop me from interrupting.

"Look at my face, Malcolm," she said in a firm voice. "Look at my eyes."

As I drew back into the living room I brushed against a lamp. All the lampshades had pompoms hanging from the edges that matched the material of the chair and the couch and that now swung in unison. In a glassed-in porch off the living room, a pygmy lime tree stood dangling small globes of unripe fruit. The house did not feel like a place that could accommodate the mess and noise of children, and I wondered what it had been like when Kevin lived there.

When I returned home that afternoon, I was rattled by the riot of objects in our trailer: Malcolm's book towers, my mother's jars of creams and bottles of lotion, the brightly colored Mexican blankets she threw over the backs of the couch and chair to hide stains. At dinner that night I did not tell Laurel about Mrs. Poole's house, or about the firm tone she took with Malcolm. Laurel would put an end to the sessions if she thought Mrs. Poole was cruel. And I didn't think that Mrs. Poole was mean. She was just demanding in a way I knew Laurel would find fault with because she didn't like people to tell her what to do. But I liked it. I felt eager around Mrs. Poole and excited about the possibility of pleasing her.

During the following days, I thought about Mrs. Poole often. I looked for her in school. I was not prepared to talk to her but when I saw her moving quietly down a corridor or heading to her car at the end of a day, my heart sped up. I couldn't explain to myself why I liked her or why the days between Malcolm's sessions began to feel long and pregnant with anticipation. She was very businesslike and did nothing to ingratiate herself to me. She was fastidious in a way that could only engender the ridicule of children, and most students I knew made fun of her. She was "uncool," as withering a personality defect as any for the kids I knew, but I wanted a place in her systematic universe. And so my attraction to her became something covert and so all the more potent.

SHE AGREED TO PAY ME two dollars an hour to weed her garden. "You need to be productive," she said the following week, when I brought Malcolm to her house, "and I have a lot of things on my plate." Before she took Malcolm inside, she showed me how to identify which plants were good and worth keeping and which were weeds that would kill her vegetables. "It takes a tremendous amount of diligence to grow these things out here. You have to fight and fight," she said, more to herself than me as she idly ran her hand over a green tomato. "These won't get anywhere on their own." She pointed out a row of beans and next to it, a row of zucchini. "It takes fortitude, really. And cunning. You have to play a trick on the desert because it will kill everything valuable." She leaned down and carefully pulled a plant out of the ground so that its roots remained intact. "This is one of the worst. It just proliferates like a virus." She held up the twiggy yellow-green plant. I knew it was cheese bush. Once, Laurel had crushed one of the spines between her fingers and held it to my nose, laughing when I reacted to the rotten scent. I had chased her, waving the bush at her, trying to force her to smell it too, and we had wrestled and screamed happily. Mrs. Poole tossed the plant onto the ground by the side of the garden. "That one is not worth saving."

At first I was uncertain which plants I should keep. I didn't want to make a mistake and disappoint Mrs. Poole, so I carefully pulled out the roots of every plant that was not a recognizable vegetable so that she could replant if I'd guessed wrong. I knew my mother would never kill these plants. She might touch them and run her fingers along their leaves the way she ran her hands over her children's heads as a way of knowing us.

At the end of Malcolm's session, Mrs. Poole frowned at the collection of plants I had laid in a neat row on the grass. "You've created more work for me," she said.

"I wasn't sure."

"You have to be sure if you're going to do the job."

I felt myself grow small.

"Tell your mother she needs to practice with Malcolm," she said, handing me a sheet of paper. "I wrote it down. Once a week isn't enough to make a difference. Your mother has to do the work at home."

I waited. "You said you were going to pay me," I said finally.

"You didn't do what I asked."

"That's not fair."

"It's exactly fair," she said. "I'm not trying to cheat you, Ares. Two dollars isn't a lot to me. But you get paid for a job well done."

On the ride home, I tried to hate her but all I could think about was what it would take to win her praise.

"Christ," Laurel said that evening when she read Mrs. Poole's note. "This is ridiculous." She laid the paper on the table and went to the cupboard. While she took out a pot and filled it with water, I read the note. *Practice normal social intercourse,* it said. *Malcolm must ask for something before he is given it. Encourage him not to grab. Encourage him to make eye contact.*

Laurel ripped open a box of spaghetti. "Normal social intercourse," she said. "It sounds like something dirty."

THE FOLLOWING WEEK, I SAT in Mrs. Poole's living room listening to her as she worked with Malcolm. Her voice was catlike, drawing back, lunging forward, pouncing when she thought she might get his attention, purring when she tried to coax him to do something. When the session was over, she handed me a typewritten list. "This might make it easier for your mother," she said.

I rode home fast, remembering only occasionally to look back to make sure Malcolm was keeping up. Once we were outside our trailer, I stood astride my bike, unfolded the list, and read.

1. *Address Malcolm by name when you talk to him. If he doesn't look you in the eyes, take his hands so he can focus on you.*
2. *Model speech. Narrate what you are doing, i.e., "I am cutting an apple. I am handing you a slice of apple." Repeat nouns with frequency. Avoid the use of "this" and "it."*
3. *When Malcolm misbehaves, i.e., grabbing, hitting, not following directions, show him your displeasure by crossing your arms and looking away from him.*

It was already dark when Laurel came home from work. Richard was with her. She glanced at the note lying on the table then walked toward her room.

"You're supposed to read it," I said, picking up the letter and following her.

"Are you a cop? Are you going to turn me in?"

"No," I said miserably. "But Mrs. Poole says . . ."

Richard took a bottle of beer out of the refrigerator. Malcolm danced around him.

"No beer for you, man," Richard said. "That'd be bad for you in ten different ways."

"It is TOO HOT!" Laurel said, emerging from her bedroom. She wore her bathing suit underneath a loose dress. "Put on your suit, Ares."

"It's already dark."

"Don't be such a downer. It's a full moon!" she said. She grabbed towels from the rack in the bathroom and fished out Malcolm's shovel and pail from underneath the couch.

Moonlight spilled on the water making it look like undulating yards of iridescent silk. On the shore, Malcolm squatted and began to dig. Laurel lifted her dress over her head, slid off her shoes, and waded into the water. The bottoms of her yellow bikini slid up between her buttocks, but she didn't bother to adjust the material. I couldn't bear to look at her body, which seemed grotesque to me. Richard stood with his hands folded over his chest, watching her with amusement as she twirled in the water. The picture of Laurel's naked breast and the forest of her pubic hair came to my mind, and I felt disgusted to think that Richard might be sharing this same private image. Laurel stood in the shallows, her hand shading her eyes as if it were the middle of a bright day. When she turned to the side, I could see the exaggerated sway of her back.

"You don't know what you're missing!" she yelled, wading farther out until she was submerged up to her waist. She held her hands out to either side of her, then suddenly brought them above her head, pitched forward, and dove. She emerged, letting out a groan of pleasure. "Come on!" she called.

"Oh, hell," Richard murmured. He stripped off his shirt, jeans, and underwear and ran naked into the water. He lunged for her and she screamed with delight.

"Ares! You too!" she called. She moved her hands in wide arcs on either side of her, brushing her fingers over the surface of the sea as if smoothing down wrinkles in a dress. "Look at this!" she said. "It's so beautiful here!"

I looked at the dry, cracking dirt by my feet, at the dead tree branches that lay scattered as if flung by Malcolm in the grip of a tantrum. "It's not beautiful to me," I said.

"What?" Laurel shouted. "I can't hear you!"

Richard tried to grab her, and she laughed and swam away from him then turned and swam back. I felt the way I did at school dances, when I stood by the wall of the gym, full of derision and jealousy for the kids who laughed and danced and seemed to know what to do with themselves. But the time when it would have been possible for me to pull off my clothes and join my mother was in the past. Laurel kicked through the shallows toward the shore. Richard followed, his penis swinging between his long legs. He toweled her off, and she even let him reach between her thighs and dry her there.

"I think I was working on a beer somewhere a while back," he said, throwing on his clothes and heading toward our trailer.

Laurel scraped her fingers through her hair. "You used to

love to swim," she said to me. She studied my face, and when her eyes traveled over my body, I became self-conscious. She smiled as if she had come to some private conclusion.

"Don't look at me like that," I said.

"Like what?"

"Like you're doing."

"Since when am I not allowed to look at you anymore?"

"It's gross."

She laughed. Malcolm walked toward us, holding a tin can that had been floating so long in the water its label was gone.

"That's a keeper," Laurel said appreciatively.

I was furious because she laughed at me, and because I felt trapped between a life I had once enjoyed and one that felt miserable and lonely and bitter. I remembered watching old war movies where the two sides marched toward each other in long lines until they reached some invisible dividing marker, at which point orders were given and guns were fired. I had not understood how a soldier could be made to walk into such certain death, but now I understood the lethal combination of anger and humiliation and fear that could make a person head toward oblivion.

"See?" I said, to an argument I needed to start. "That water's a garbage dump. You're going to get some disease in there."

"The world's a garbage dump," she said, folding the towels. "But there is beauty, right Mal? Malcolm knows."

"Knows what?"

"He knows about beauty in unlikely places."

"How do you know he knows about that?"

She looked at me warily. "I just do."

"What if he doesn't?"

"What do you mean?"

"I mean what you're talking about." My mind stumbled over the enormous boulders of mistakes strewn in this path I'd committed to. "Maybe that's not what he's thinking."

She stared at me, but I could tell she wasn't seeing me. She was seeing something else, maybe a baby lying on the concrete ground of a gas station. Her faced closed in on itself, and I knew I had hurt her.

"What if you're wrong?" I said, unable to stop myself. "What if you're wrong about him?"

"I'm sure I'm wrong about most things," she said sharply. "Isn't that what Mrs. Poole says? All those *notes?*" She leaned over and picked up Malcolm's sand toys then wriggled her shoes onto her sandy feet. She took Malcolm's hand and they walked back toward town. I was left alone, my anger unspent, the adrenaline from my first overt act of rebellion making me jittery. I went home, found my bike, and rode out to the drainage ditch where I'd buried the gun. I did not dig it up, but it made me feel good to be near something that had the potential to make me powerful. I heard the muted sound of an explosion, and in the far distance, at the foot of the Chocolate Mountains, I saw the sky flare and then dim, and I knew they were dropping bombs at the training ground. How I wished I was there, among those soldiers and those sounds and all that destruction.

When it was fully dark, with nowhere else to go, I returned home. Richard was gone. Laurel stood by the stove with her back to me. When she turned, I could tell she'd been crying.

"What happened to Richard?"

"Yes. Exactly. What *did* happen to him?" she said sarcastically. But her tears were starting again. "What an asshole."

"What did he do?"

"Nothing. He does nothing. Mistakes don't just *happen*, right? People make them. He takes no responsibility for what he does. You have to take some goddamn responsibility in this life. Do you know that?" She searched my face, and I wondered if she was talking about Richard or me.

She turned back to the stove, lifted a pan of scrambled eggs, and carried it over to the table.

"The knob," I said. "You forgot to turn off the knob."

She slammed the pan down on the table, left it there, and turned off the burner. Something began to smell sweet and smoky.

"Lift it up!" she said.

"What?"

"The pan! Lift it up!" she repeated, rushing toward me. She picked up the pan and stared at the mark burned into the table.

"It's not my fault," I said reflexively.

"Oh, shit," she said, her tears running over her cheeks.

During dinner, she ate little and stared distractedly away from the table toward the blank television screen. The silence of the meal was punctuated only by Malcolm's occasional sounds and the clatter of dishware. When his plate was empty she gave him two more slices of bread. When he finished those, she gave him another.

"Shouldn't he stop?" I said.

"What?"

"He's had five pieces of bread."

"He's hungry."

"I thought we were supposed to—"

"Oh, God!" she exclaimed. "I'm so tired of all these rules. I don't care what that lady says."

"It's what you say."

She dismissed me with a wave of her hand.

"Want to play?" I said to Malcolm, standing up and trying to distract him from the food, and Laurel from whatever internal conversation was making her forget how to care for him. "We can do World War One bombers," I said. "Or African explorers." I cleared his plate. He held on to my arm to stop me, but I didn't give in, and he moaned. Laurel stood and reached into a high cupboard, producing a package of ginger snaps I didn't even know was there. She poured the wafers onto a plate and put it in the middle of the table.

"Isn't this sugar?" I said.

"I need a little sugar today, okay? *I* need it. So we all get sugar. It's not going to kill us." She lit one of her clove cigarettes, took a drag, then stubbed it out. "I'm going to lie down. Don't bother me." She headed toward her bedroom.

"It's a bath night."

She wheeled around. "I just can't do this by myself," she said, her voice pitched as if we were in the midst of an argument. "I can't."

"What?"

"This," she said, waving her arm to include the trailer, Malcolm, and me. "It's too much! I'm just one person, okay?"

"I'll do it. I'll give him a bath," I said as she disappeared behind her card curtain.

After the fifth cookie, Malcolm started to bounce around so I took him outside. We ran up and down the street pretending we were Special Forces infiltrating Vietcong strongholds until Malcolm was so tired he fell to the ground. I lifted him up and carried him home.

Laurel was already asleep. I watched her through the openings between the strands of cards. She had passed out in the clothes she had been wearing and had not even taken the time to get under the covers as if her need to disappear into unconsciousness had been urgent. I didn't know what had happened between her and Richard. I assumed it had to do with me and what I had said to her on the beach, although if someone had asked me to explain why I thought so, I would not have been able to tell them. But I was used to construing truth out of meaningful looks and unsaid words, and I needed no proof or logic to convince myself that I was at the root of her unhappiness.

NINE

Mrs. Poole handed me a pamphlet called *Plants of the Southern California Desert*. "Anything in there, you throw out," she said.

While she worked with Malcolm in the kitchen, I sat on the front porch and studied the guide. There were black and white drawings of plants along with descriptions and maps that showed where the plants were likely to grow. I read about iodine bush and greenfire, about wild grape and bedstraw—all plants I'd heard my mother name. I carried the pamphlet to the garden and slowly began to try to match the plants in the book with the ones that sprouted between and around the rows of vegetables. By the end of the hour, I had made a small, neat pile of the weeds and grasses I was pretty certain were the viruses Mrs. Poole had spoken about. I wondered if she thought Malcolm had a virus and that if she pulled it out of him he would be better. I hoped she could do it but not too quickly, because Mrs. Poole's house was beginning to feel like a respite from my own, which had lately become heavy with the dark weather of Laurel's unhappiness. She moved from one activity to the next with a kind of remoteness, as if half of her was paying attention to a conversation that was taking place only in her mind.

In among the discarded weeds lay a saltbush plant. This was one of Laurel's favorites. She had shown me the sharp spine and the delicate flowers. I picked up the plant, trying to see what my mother admired about the lank and dusty thing just as Mrs. Poole came around the corner of the house followed by Malcolm. She placed her hand on his shoulder. To my surprise, he did not react badly. She smiled proudly.

"No session next week," she said.

"Why not?" I was disappointed by the news and because she took no notice of my work.

"I will be out of town on Friday. Let your mother know."

"What about the library?"

She laughed. "You should run the school! I've arranged for a substitute." She glanced at the garden. "You've done a good job today, Ares. I'm pleased." She handed me two single dollar bills and a note for my mother.

On the bike ride home, I stood on my pedals and reached into my pocket. The dollar bills were warm and soft like a puppy's ear.

DURING THE NEXT TWO WEEKS, the atmosphere at home pulsed with the energy of things unsaid. Laurel came home from work, made dinner, and lay down on her bed. Richard came around to see us, and some nights she went to Slab City to see him, but she found no occasion to take us walking in the desert or swimming in the sea. She told us she was sick and not to make noise because her head hurt. She was irritable, yelling at us when we made a mess with the pillows on the couch, or when I left my shoes lying around, which I had always done, and which she had never minded before, but which now represented a number of character deficits including lack of respect for her, treating the house like a garbage dump, disregard for how much things cost, and general thoughtlessness. Occasionally she would play with Malcolm, but where she once had endless patience to help him make his piles or to read him books he did not pay attention to, now she quickly lost interest and ended up sitting next to him silently, fingering his hair, staring at the walls or at her hands. Her depression hovered watchfully above us at all times so that it felt like a betrayal to smile or laugh. My time at home began to feel like time in a prison cell. The smells of Laurel's flowery shampoo, the grainy sweetness of her slow-cooked oatmeal, Malcolm's heedless farts—all of these things made me want to erupt. My room began to smell different too: sharp and sweet and rancid at the same time. I bathed each morning and evening to try to rid myself of this new odor, but whenever I crawled into bed each night, and especially after I masturbated, that smell was there again, clinging to me.

My desire to please Mrs. Poole filled my body with extra air and made me feel that I was too big for my skin. This enormous feeling's proximity to its own extinction made me experience a continuous, pleasurable anxiety. Sometimes, when she passed me in the school hallway, she looked at me blankly as if she didn't recognize me. But other times she would say hello or pat me on the shoulder. She had a particular smell that wasn't apparent at first but only surfaced after being in her presence a while, at which point a powdery, clean scent floated toward me as if hovering not in the air but somehow on top of it like a cloud. I was certain that none of the other boys at school could smell this perfume and I was proud of my secret. When she smiled at me, I felt like a bug with a foot suspended over it; I knew something darker and obliterating would follow. When she took away that smile, I felt an aching humiliation, like when the teacher asked for my homework and then watched with silent condemnation while I searched in the trash bin of my backpack for the nonexistent paper.

I WAS FILLED WITH A giddy excitement when we returned to her house two weeks later.

"The garden needs help," she said when she greeted us at her door. "But get your homework done first." She ushered me into the living room then joined Malcolm in the kitchen. I listened to her familiar words as she alternated between stern directives and playful cajoling. Malcolm did something right and she offered him his choice of reward: a peanut butter cracker or a Slim Jim.

I studied her bookshelf, which was dominated by a set of classic books bound in leather. I scanned the titles—*The Good Earth, Vanity Fair, David Copperfield* among them—recognizing how much there was to know and how little of it

I had mastered. There were also some big hardback novels by Irving Wallace, the edges of the yellowing jackets peeling like Band-Aids left on too long. Books about marine wildlife nearly filled an entire shelf. Four photo albums filled in the rest of the space. I opened one and paged through it. The photos were taken long ago. Mrs. Poole looked younger, almost like a girl, her face unlined, her smile hopeful as if the future were a gift she was about to open. In one shot, she stood with her then beardless husband on a fishing boat. Mrs. Poole, grimacing, held a big fish by a hook, leaning away from it as if she thought it was still alive and might bite her. Her hair was caught in a red scarf, the ends of which flew out in the wind like a kite's tail. There were other pictures of Mr. and Mrs. Poole in places I didn't recognize— green places with lawns and leafy trees that cast shadows at their feet. I turned to a page full of pictures of Mrs. Poole cooking at an outdoor barbecue, of the couple in a convertible waving, of Mrs. Poole coming out of a camp tent, her hair messy, her shirt held together with one hand, her other hand held out toward the camera to stop it from seeing what it saw. There was a shot of her lying on a beach—a wide, sandy expanse unlike our own—wearing shorts and a blouse. She held the blouse up so that her pale stomach was exposed to the sun. A strip of black bra peeked out from underneath the bunched-up shirt.

"Finish your work?" She stood in the opening between the kitchen and the living room. She stared at the book in my hands.

"Yes," I said, feeling heat rise up my face.

"You're welcome to borrow any book you like," she said, coming toward me. "As long as you ask first and return it promptly."

I could barely look at her. Perhaps she had known about *The Gold and Gods of Peru* all along. Maybe she had been waiting for the best possible moment to humiliate me, and now, with my hands on a picture of her practically naked body, she had found it.

She took the photo album from me, closed it, and replaced it on the shelf. She straightened all the albums so they stood at attention, their edges flush with the wood. Then, as if on a whim, she took another album off the shelf and opened the pages to snapshots of her, her husband, and Kevin. Both parents flanked the boy, all three looking as if they were in a police lineup.

"We visited him. That's where we went last week," she said, staring at the pictures. "Usually we go on Sundays, but . . ." she drifted off. "He looked . . . healthy," she continued, rejoining her thought somewhere down the line. "He gained a little weight. He says the food is pretty good, actually." She closed the album and put it carefully next to the others. "Well, I'm not much for cooking anyway, so I imagine he's getting better food there than here," she added.

Malcolm appeared at the door.

"Finished your treat?" Mrs. Poole said, brightening. Her face opened into that rare, generous smile, and for the first time I realized that she truly liked my brother, and I dared to believe she liked me too. He opened his mouth. Bits of brown were stuck in his teeth. She went to him and put her arm

THE GOD OF WAR | 119

around his shoulders. "Who doesn't like Slim Jims, huh?" she said, leading him into the kitchen.

THE NEXT WEEK, I STOOD alone at her door. "Malcolm is sick," I said when she opened it.

"You didn't have to come all the way out here to tell me that," she said. She was barefoot. Her toenails were painted a surprising orange. "You could have just come to the library."

"I forgot."

"You should remember those kinds of things. Then you don't have to waste your time."

"I don't mind."

She began to shut the door.

"My mom had to take him to work with her," I said quickly, trying to hold her attention.

"I hope he had a chance to rest."

"There's lots of beds there," I said, and when she looked confused, I told her about the spa, because mentioning beds made me feel like I had said something unseemly.

"Well, I hope Malcolm gets better soon." She moved once again to shut the door but stopped when she realized I wasn't leaving. "Do you need something?"

"I thought . . . the garden," I said.

"My husband got enthusiastic this weekend, so I think we're in pretty good shape for now."

"Oh."

"I can't invent work that doesn't exist, Ares."

"I'm not asking you to."

"You were looking forward to getting paid."

"It's only two dollars."

"Only two?" she laughed. "I thought I made you a good deal."

"You did."

"I guess two dollars doesn't mean a whole lot anymore," she said to herself. "Everything's so out of proportion."

"Out of proportion to what?"

"To my expectations, I guess," she said. "But I suppose I've always been a little naive."

I didn't know what she meant but I didn't want the conversation to end. "I'm thirsty."

"Alright," she said. "You can drink Malcolm's juice. I've already poured it out anyway."

For the first time, I sat at her kitchen table. She had laid out the flash cards and wooden shapes she used with Malcolm along with a glass of juice. She had emptied a box of animal crackers onto a plate and arranged the animals in a line. None of the cookies were broken. She must have gone through the box and discarded the monkeys without tails and the lions with no heads. I picked out a tiger cookie and bit off a paw.

"Kevin used to bite off the feet first just like that," she said. "Then the tail, then the head. He saved the body for last."

" 'Cause the body's the biggest part. It has the most cookie."

"I'm not sure that much theory was involved as far as Kevin was concerned. He's more the impulsive type. Like most boys, I suppose. It took me a while to get used to it. Maybe you're different."

"I'm not different."

"There's nothing wrong with being different."

"How old is he?"

"Fifteen."

"He probably doesn't eat animal cookies anymore."

"Oh, he'll eat a box if I buy them," she said. "Some things you never grow out of."

I couldn't think of anything else to say so I ate in silence, my eyes roving the room as I slowly chewed. One of the kitchen cabinets stood ajar, and I could see that the shelves were lined with boxes of many different kinds of cereal. The idea that she thought about the future when she went shopping was strange and spoke to me of a life so different from my own. Laurel shopped meal by meal. Sometimes we went to the store and she would stand in an aisle, staring at the stacks of food on the shelves. "So, what do we feel like?" she'd say, as if our choices were limitless and we could have roast beef any day of the week.

A lazy Susan dominated the middle of the kitchen table. The only other time I'd seen one was when Sam, Malcolm's father, took me and my mother to the Chinese restaurant in Palm Springs where he worked as a prep cook. A sugar bowl, salt and pepper shakers, and a basket holding steak sauces sat on the raised center of Mrs. Poole's lazy Susan. I wanted to spin the big circular disk to see how fast it would go. I wondered if this was something Kevin did, if this was something he and I shared.

"Is he coming home soon?" I asked.

"Who?"

"Your son."

She breathed in sharply. "You're interested in Kevin, aren't you?"

"Not really."

"Kids are. Mostly for the wrong reasons." She pushed back her chair and stood up. Reluctantly, I followed her to the door, angry at myself for ending our time together.

"You ought to stand your bike up," she said, looking at my bicycle, which lay on her walkway. "It's bad for the gears."

"It doesn't have a kickstand."

"You should get one. They're not expensive."

"Okay. I will."

She laughed lightly. "You're very agreeable."

"Not really."

"It's a compliment."

"At home I'm not so nice all the time."

"Well, home can be a complicated place."

"It doesn't seem complicated here."

She looked at me carefully, seemed to hesitate, then spoke. "Would you like to meet Kevin?"

"Sure."

"I'm going to visit him on Sunday. You can come along if you'd like. I think he'd enjoy seeing a new face."

"Okay."

"You have to ask your mother if it's alright with her."

"She won't mind."

"Ask her."

"I will."

"I'll call your house to confirm."

"She works," I said quickly. "She's never home."

"Not even at night?"

"She's tired. She doesn't like to talk on the phone."

"Well, I'll need a note."

I nodded, already imagining copying Laurel's signature, the wide loop of her *L* dwarfing the other letters, which looked like small goslings following their long-necked mother.

"I told Kevin about you. You and your brother. I like him to know what's going on here. I want to keep him involved in our life."

"He knows my name?"

She smiled. "He thought it was an interesting name."

"It's the god of war. It's from myths."

"Yes, I know."

"I'm not really interested in war, though. I used to be when I was little. But not anymore. My mom doesn't let us play with guns."

"I should hope not."

"I mean toy guns."

"Well, you never know around here."

"I make them out of sticks. I mean I used to. Not anymore."

"You boys and your guns. I don't know what the fascination is."

"But I don't have a gun," I said, feeling as though somehow she knew the secret of my buried treasure.

"I know," she said, laughing, her eyes lighting up. "I was just teasing you." She ruffled my hair.

That Sunday, I told Laurel I was going to ride my bike. As I expected, she didn't question me. Malcolm still had a fever, and she wasn't feeling well either. She said it was probably a good idea for me to get out of the house rather than go stir crazy staring at two sick people, and she gave me a few dollars in case I got hungry. I put the money into the pocket of my jeans next to my forged note.

"Maybe tonight I'll feel better. We can play Monopoly."

"Okay."

She smiled wanly and rested her chin on top of Malcolm's head.

THE JUVENILE DETENTION CENTER WAS forty-five minutes from Mrs. Poole's house. I rode in the passenger seat of her Oldsmobile station wagon. She placed two cans of Coke between us on the front seat along with a pack of peanut butter crackers and a napkin. "We'll eat lunch with Kevin," she said when we got into the car. "The crackers will tide you over."

We drove in silence. She stared at the road, occasionally flexing a tired hand. I ate the crackers, twisting apart the two halves and scraping the peanut butter off with my teeth. I was careful to eat the crackers in one bite so that crumbs wouldn't fall over the clean car upholstery. Still, a few bits fell onto my lap. After I gathered them up, I was not sure what to do. Eating them would provide another opportunity to make a mess, and it might appear to her as though I was eating trash. So I held them in my fist for the rest of the ride, letting them fall to the ground after we parked and got out of the car.

My expectation of the prison and its reality diverged so radically that, for a moment, I thought I had misunderstood, and that we were not going to be visiting Kevin at all, but that Mrs. Poole had taken me to a department store. I had imagined a block of drab, windowless government buildings surrounded by cyclone fencing, and guard towers with dour-faced sentinels in sunglasses standing inside them, slowly scanning the prison yard, rifles at the ready. But the detention center turned out to be one of the most modern and bright-looking buildings I'd ever seen. It stood out in the landscape as something impervious to the battery of sun and wind. It seemed optimistic and enduring in a way very few buildings in the desert did. The structure was all curves—an architectural style that was new and startling to eyes used to utilitarian squares and rectangles. Purple and yellow decorative stripes wrapped around its middle like ribbons on a present. There were many floor-to-ceiling windows that revealed the reception area within.

"They have an indoor tree!" I blurted out.

"What?" she said distractedly as we walked across the parking lot toward the main entrance.

"A tree. It's growing inside the building."

"I guess it is. I never really thought about it."

"Is there a hole in the ceiling?"

"What?"

"For the tree. To get out at the top."

"I suppose. I don't know. I really don't know anything about the tree, Ares," she said sharply. She adjusted the belt on her dress, touched her hair, then gripped the shoulder strap on her purse so hard her fingers became bloodless. A small brass sign next to the front door read: "Oak Glen Juvenile Improvement Center." The name made me think the detention center was more like a camp, a place where you could get better at things like swimming or basketball, or making bracelets out of lanyard. Inside, the reception area was decorated with framed posters of baby animals and flowers. Magazines were stacked neatly on small laminated tables, which were in turn surrounded by comfortable couches and chairs. Mrs. Poole instructed me to take a seat while she signed in. There was a small area to the left of the couches covered in red and yellow rubber mats. Two little children negotiated a plastic climbing structure and slid down the two-foot slide. They were too big to get up much speed, but they went at the activity over and over again.

"Here, put this on," Mrs. Poole said, walking toward me and handing me a tag on which she had written my name in her perfect librarian cursive. The fact of her having considered the letters that formed my name felt thrilling and intimate to me.

"Follow me," she said. She led me through a metal detector, then to a closed door, where she stopped and waited. I heard a click and the door seemed to unlock itself. Mrs. Poole pushed it open, and I followed her into a short corridor. A security camera stared down at us from the ceiling. I made sure to keep my hands by my side. I didn't want to forget myself and scratch my nose or make a sudden suspicious movement. The hallway led to another door. Mrs. Poole stopped again, waited for the click, and I followed her out into a fenced yard.

Made of hard-packed dirt interspersed with concrete playing surfaces, the yard was full of boys standing in clusters, all wearing identical dark blue pants and white T-shirts. There was a half court, and next to that a set of chinning bars. Across the yard, by the far fence, stood a row of high swinging rings. Some boys took turns on the rings, launching themselves expertly from one to the next. Others kicked a soccer ball or played basketball. Mrs. Poole tilted her chin up and looked across the yard of boys, smiling tensely as though she expected a ball to hit her in the face. She waved hesitantly. A boy pulled away from the group standing near the rings and started toward us. He was tall and lanky, and his light brown hair was cut into a short brush like all the other boys. His walk was indolent; he practically slithered, barely lifting his feet off the ground as if any decisive movement might reveal too much desire. Kevin looked younger than he did in the picture on Mrs. Poole's desk in the library. His ears stuck out on either side of his face like the handles on a jug, and the tips were sunburned a deep red. His high color helped obscure his acne. Mrs. Poole smiled, but he didn't smile back. She reached out and patted him awkwardly on the shoulder.

"You look like you got too much sun," she said. "Don't they give you sun lotion?"

"No," he said. He stared down at the ground, put his hands in his pockets.

"Well, I'm going to say something about that," she said. "This sun is punishing. Even for the darker boys."

Kevin looked me over. I felt short and embarrassed to have no discernible muscles like the boys around me. I did not in any way resemble someone who could have done anything brave enough to be in this place.

"This is Ares, the boy I told you about. The one with the brother I work with at the house," she said. "He asked if he could come. He wanted to meet you."

Her white lie and her surprising nervousness around her son made me think that she had invited me to act as a buffer between them.

"Hey," Kevin said.

"Hi." I raised my hand but then let it drop, feeling foolish.

"Jerry had to go to a meeting," she said. "On a weekend no less. He said to say he's sorry he couldn't make it."

"No he didn't," Kevin said, without apparent rancor. "He never comes."

"You know his work is demanding."

Kevin shrugged off the excuse. "I don't care if he comes or not. I don't care if you come."

They were silent for a while. Kevin stared at the ground. Mrs. Poole looked across the yard then back. "Did you have a good week?"

"I hate it here."

"How were the classes?"

He shrugged. "They're doing stuff I already know."

"I guess they have to account for all the boys in here. Some of them might not have had much schooling."

"Some of them are idiots. Real retards."

"Well, we shouldn't judge."

"I knew you'd say that."

Her face colored. "School is school, right?" she said, trying to recover. She continued talking about things that didn't matter, like the weather and how many times a week Kevin was allowed to shower. Her efforts were embarrassing. I wondered if she was keeping the conversation going for my benefit or whether, on normal visits, they had anything to say to each other at all.

"How is the therapy going?" she said.

"It's for faggots."

She absorbed this. "Have you had a chance to talk yet?"

Something flashed in his eyes that was kin to a smile but wasn't. "Yeah. Sure. All the time."

"What do you talk about?" she said.

"I don't have to tell you."

"Of course not. I just—"

"I told them that I hit you. That I gave you a black eye. That I practically broke your nose."

She glanced at me, clearly upset that I had heard this. "I just want you to get the help you need."

Kevin looked over his shoulder at a passing group of kids. I could tell he wanted to be with them, not stuck here with his mother, whom he didn't seem to like at all. A noise erupted from the boys standing near the rings.

"What's going on?" she said, with a manufactured enthusiasm. She was acting the way adults did at zoos when
they tried to get children excited about watching crocodiles
that never moved. "Let's go over and see. I hope no one has
overtaken your record. Tell Ares about the record."

"It's nothing," Kevin mumbled.

"It's not nothing," Mrs. Poole said. "Tell him."

"I did a hundred once," Kevin said, following her toward
the rings.

"Well," Mrs. Poole corrected him, "fifty times one way,
fifty times the other. You should see Kevin on the rings. He
moves like invisible wires are holding him up. He's very
good at gymnastics but he won't take it at school." We
stopped near the apparatus. "Kevin, show Ares."

"No thanks."

"Ares would like to see, wouldn't you, Ares?"

I felt trapped. I was mesmerized by Kevin, by the evident
power of his apathy. He was like a boat rocking unevenly beneath Mrs. Poole, making her unsure of her footing. His
power over her was almost frightening to witness. It had
never before occurred to me that I could gain some dominion
over my life by doing the very opposite of what I had learned
to do all these years. I could disregard what Laurel thought
of me. I could simply not care.

"Wouldn't you like to see, Ares?" Mrs. Poole repeated,
more desperately.

"I guess."

Reluctantly, Kevin took his place in line, becoming quickly
absorbed in the conversation of the boys there. When it was

his turn, Mrs. Poole put a hand on my shoulder. "Watch," she said.

Another boy stood behind Kevin and helped him jump up and reach the rings. Once Kevin got a firm grip, he jack-knifed his legs back and forth several times to gain momentum then reached for the second ring. I heard the slap of his hand connecting to the metal as he glided from one ring to the next all the way down the line.

"It takes a lot of upper body strength," Mrs. Poole said, not taking her eyes off her son.

Kevin reached the end of the line then smoothly turned himself around and started back. He faltered midway through, missed a ring, and had to swing himself a few times to get his rhythm back.

Mrs. Poole's expression tightened as she watched him. When he gained the next ring, she looked away. "Well, it's hard to be put on the spot," she said.

When Kevin finished, he walked toward us, staring at his open palms, which were red and puffy.

"Great job," Mrs. Poole said, smiling enthusiastically.

"Yeah," I said. "That was cool."

"Thanks," he mumbled.

We ate lunch in the cafeteria. There were a lot of visitors eating with boys, and the atmosphere was lively. Several men wearing badges that said "Monitor" on them stood at the perimeter of the room, walkie-talkies hanging from their belts. A group of boys became rowdy. When one of them stood up and leaned across the table to make his point, a monitor pushed off the wall and started toward the commotion, walking slowly and deliberately. He stopped about six feet from the table, his legs spread in an upside-down V, his hands folded in front of his groin. The boy sat down, grew quiet, and stared at his plate.

We ate our hamburgers in silence. Mrs. Poole looked tired and seemed to have lost her earlier optimism. She ate small bites, then finally gave up. Kevin finished his burger in a matter of minutes, not taking his eyes off his meal as if he thought it would be stolen out from under him unless he was vigilant and quick. I shook a bottle of ketchup over my burger and some of the paste flew onto Kevin's shirt.

"What the fuck?" he said, standing up, his expression instantly twisted with rage.

"Sorry," I said, mortified.

Mrs. Poole held her hands out toward Kevin and turned her face away from him, as if she were protecting herself. "Oh," she said. "Oh, no."

"Shit's all over my shirt! Do you see this?" he shouted, holding his shirt toward her. "Do you see this shit he did?"

"It's okay," she said, dropping her arms, trying to regain her composure. "Take a breath." People at other tables looked in our direction. One of the monitors walked toward us.

"Why'd you do that, man?" Kevin said to me. "What's your fucking problem?"

"It was a mistake," Mrs. Poole said.

"I'm sorry," I repeated miserably.

"Is there a problem here?" the monitor said.

"We're okay," Mrs. Poole said. "It was just an accident."

"Sit down, Kevin," the man said, and Kevin obeyed. "Can you get control of yourself?"

"Yes, sir," Kevin said quietly.

"Do you need some time alone?"

From Kevin's reaction, I had the feeling this meant something different and more upsetting than Kevin taking some peaceful moments in his room.

"No, sir," Kevin said. "I am in control of myself, sir. I'm overreacting, sir."

"Who do you need to tell that to?"

Kevin, with some reluctance, faced me. "I overreacted," he said. "I apologize for my behavior."

"Are we going to have anymore problems here?" the man said.

"No, sir," Kevin answered.

The monitor nodded once and returned to his position at the wall.

After lunch, we followed Kevin to his cottage. It was decorated like an army barracks. Six low metal beds were lined up against one wall. The beds were all made up exactly the same way, the sheets pulled tight around the mattresses, the blankets folded down evenly. Each boy had a footlocker and a small side table, but there were no personal items on these tables, only identical drinking cups.

Kevin opened his locker and took out a fresh shirt. He turned away from us and pulled his soiled shirt over his head. The developing muscles of his back undulated. A long red scratch ran alongside his spine.

"What happened to your back?" Mrs. Poole said, concerned. "Did someone hurt you?"

"We were just fooling around. It's nothing."

"It's not nothing," she said. She stepped toward him and touched the injury lightly. "It looks infected. Did someone examine this?"

He spun around. "Don't," he said.

She shrank back. "I just . . . I just . . ."

"Don't act like you give a shit," he said. He pulled on the clean shirt.

"Kevin, don't do that. Don't push me away. I'm trying to help you. Haven't you talked about this in therapy?"

He looked at her evenly. "Visiting day is over."

MRS. POOLE KEPT THE WINDOWS open during the drive home, and a hot wind blew into the car. She drove with both hands on the wheel, leaning forward in her seat as if she thought it would get her home faster.

"It's a pretty good place for a prison," I said.

She looked at me in alarm. "Prison? What are you talking about? He's not in prison."

"I just thought . . . The kids at school said . . ."

"The kids at school," she said unkindly. "It's not a prison. It's a residential treatment center. He's receiving help there."

"What's wrong with him?"

"He's had a different kind of life from you, Ares," she said. "It's too hard for you to understand."

"Sorry."

"It's not a prison," she said again.

When she pulled into her driveway, she didn't leave the car or indicate that she wanted me to get out, so I stayed. The front door opened, and Mr. Poole walked toward us. He wore a tie knotted loosely and the sleeves of his shirt were rolled up revealing tanned and ropy forearms. He wore hiking boots, and despite his shirt and tie, he looked like someone more at home camping out than in an office. He shook his glasses open and put them on.

"Why doesn't Kevin call him 'Dad'?" I said.

"Kevin is our foster child."

Mr. Poole leaned into the driver's side window. "Long drive?" he said.

She nodded in a way that included a whole complicated answer to that question.

"How's he doing?" he said.

"You should visit him and find out," she said sharply.

"I had a meeting."

She pressed her lips together as if to stop from saying the wrong thing. "His therapists gave him a good report. He'll be able to come home soon."

"Let's not jump the gun."

"He would be better off at home, not at an institution. We are not giving up on him."

Mr. Poole glanced at me, then back to his wife. "We'll talk about this later," he said.

Riding home on my bike, I thought about the photograph albums in Mrs. Poole's house and about how there were no pictures of Kevin as a baby or a little boy. Laurel kept all her

photographs in shoeboxes, which I pawed through on occasion, mystified by the acts of banality and outright humiliation (me at a year, peeing an exuberant arc into the air) she
had chosen to cement in time. In most of Mrs. Poole's photographs, Kevin squinted into the sun, one hand shielding his
brow as if Mr. or Mrs. Poole had forced him to take off his
hat so that they could see his face. In those pictures, Kevin
looked like he was reacting to a splinter.

TEN

A week later, Laurel was dressing for a rare evening out. We were all going to meet Richard at the Slab City Talent Show. "I'm not up for this," Laurel said. She was half-dressed in a flowery Mexican skirt and her bra. She stood in the bathroom putting on makeup, something I had rarely seen her do. She stared at herself in the mirror to take in the effect. She smiled, then drew her lips into an exaggerated kiss, then seemed to give up on something and wiped the lipstick off her mouth with the back of her hand. Malcolm sat at the table, coloring with crayons. He made bold, angry gestures across the paper, layering color upon color. I showed him how to take the point of a pen and trace a design into the thick wax. He tore a gash down the center of his drawing.

"I'm going to lie down," Laurel said, coming out of the bathroom. "Wake me up in fifteen minutes."

"Are you still sick? Maybe you should go to the doctor."

"I'm just tired."

"You're always tired." I heard the edge in my voice. I

wanted to shake her out of her depression. Or maybe I just wanted to fight.

"For God's sake, Ares," she said, exasperated. She headed toward her room.

"And you're always going into your room."

"I just need a little space."

"You come home every night and all you want to do is get away from us."

"Maybe you're the one who wants to get away. You're picking this fight, not me. I just want to lie down before we go out tonight. Help your brother out," she said, going into her room and letting the curtain fall behind her. "He wants something."

I looked over to see Malcolm standing in front of the refrigerator. "Tell me what you want," I said. I opened the refrigerator and took out a carton of juice and an apple. "Don't grab. Just tell." I danced away from him as he reached for the apple. He let out a wail.

"What's going on?" Laurel called out.

"Nothing."

But Malcolm made another unhappy sound, and she pushed through the card curtain. "What are you doing?" she demanded.

"We're practicing."

"Practicing what?"

"What he's supposed to do."

Malcolm reached for the apple again.

"No," I said, pulling the apple away from him. "You want an apple? You have to tell me."

"Cut it out," Laurel said evenly.

"Come on, Mal," I said, ignoring her.

"I said stop it!" She pushed me out of the way and took the apple from my hand, rinsed it under the faucet, and handed it to Malcolm.

"That's not the way you're supposed to do it," I said.

"And what does your Mrs. Poole say is the way I am supposed to talk to my own child?"

"He does it right at her house," I said. "He points sometimes."

"Tricks," she said. "She's teaching him tricks. Like a goddamn dog. Well, fine. If that's what it takes for them to keep him in that classroom, so that I can go to work, so that I can make money, so that we can eat and have a life, and I can take care of all the . . . all the *shit* that it's up to me to take care of, I'll play along. Because right now, I have more to deal with than I can manage."

"She's helping him."

"Really? Is she going to stick around when things get rough for Mal? He's got a whole life ahead of him. He's going to be a teenager and then a man. Is she going to be there to help him when he's a man? Is she going to love him the way we do?"

"She's not his mother."

"That's right," Laurel said. "I'm his mother. You are his brother. Malcolm is ours. Yours and mine. We brought him into this world."

"I didn't."

"Do you see the way he looks at you? You are everything to him."

"He doesn't look at me. Sometimes he doesn't even know I'm there."

"Don't say that."

"It's true. You don't want to admit it, but it's true."

She stared at me. "You break my heart, you know that?"

"I don't care."

I watched her receive the blow of my indifference. The wound weakened her. I felt an angry gratification.

The talent show took place inside the Slab City Bar. The semipermanent structure was decorated with a reckless combination of objects. Wagon wheels were nailed to the walls along with old movie posters. A fake stuffed King Kong hung from one corner holding a Barbie doll in his hairy fist. Giant Chinese fans decorated the wall behind the bar.

Laurel's skirt, studded with sequins, flashed in the lights of the room. Her cheeks shined with makeup. She stood at the bar with Richard, holding on to his arm as he ordered a beer for himself, 7Up for me and Malcolm. I was impressed by the burly bartender, whose mustache hung down on either side of his chin like an elongated frown.

The talent show was short. A woman wearing a long red dress sang *There's got to be a morning after*... Another woman in a cowboy shirt sang "I Am Woman," but she got booed from the stage before she finished. An older couple sang "Moon River." The woman's blond hair was teased into the shape of a soft ice cream cone. Her partner played the saw, which sounded wobbly and sad as if it were crying, and the whole room grew silent.

"They're pretty good," Laurel said, applauding when the act was over. "I wonder if they were somebody once."

"Everyone was somebody once," Richard said, leading her to the dance floor. She danced sinuously, writhing her shoulders and leaning back so that the white curve of her throat was exposed. I cringed when I saw men eyeing her with interest. When she spun, her skirt fanned out around her, exposing her thighs. After a few songs, Richard left her on the dance floor to get a drink at the bar. She stayed where she was, eyes closed, swaying to the music. A biker started to dance close to her, trying to get her to open her eyes and acknowledge him, but when she didn't, he gave up and moved away. Richard appeared at our table with a bowl of chips and two more 7Ups, one of which he put in front of Mal.

"I don't think he should have any more soda," I said.

" 'Should' is a no-no word tonight," he said as Malcolm slipped the straw into his mouth and began to inhale the drink. "A night like this is definitely for should-nots."

"Maybe we should ask my mom."

"Let her be," he said, looking at Laurel dancing her private dance. "Just one night, let your old lady have some fun."

"Dust in the Wind" started playing, and Richard returned to the dance floor. I tried to take Malcolm's drink from him, but he made noises, and I didn't want to risk a scene. Laurel broke away from Richard and waved her hands in front of his face. At first, I thought they were just going to do a fast dance but then I realized they were fighting. Laurel's voice rose above the music, and other dancers looked at her. Richard tried to grab her arm, but she shook him off. A moment later, she pushed through the crowd and walked outside, and he followed. As Malcolm got down from his stool to go to her, he knocked over his glass. Soda and ice slid across the rutted wood table and spilled on his pants. I lifted the glass and tried to push the rest of the liquid away from the lip of the table, but he was already soaked. He began to hum and rock. Between the spill and the sugar, I knew what was coming. I tried to steer him to the door, but he was too immersed in his anxiety to move.

"Come on, Mal," I whispered.

He flapped his arms and hummed loudly. People stopped what they were doing and watched. Some backed away. When I tried to grab him, he let out a piercing shriek.

The bartender appeared next to me. "You get him out of here now," he said. "I could get shut down for having minors in here in the first place, not to mention he's drunk."

"He's not drunk," I said.

"Where's your folks at?" the man said, scanning the crowd. "Christ. Who's responsible here?"

Malcolm erupted again with a sound that was like an arrow headed straight for the eardrum.

"Jesus Christ," the bartender said.

I put my hands on either side of Malcolm's face. "Let's count. One, two, three . . ."

"You need to get out of here right now," the bartender said, gripping me hard on my arm.

"Four, five, six . . ." I continued, whispering into Malcolm's hair.

"Okay," the bartender said, making a decision. He picked up Malcolm and hoisted him over his shoulder. I caught sight of my brother's face as he was carried toward the door. His mouth was stretched open but no sound came out. His eyes were huge.

"Get off him!" I yelled. "Put him down!"

The bartender didn't stop.

"He's not drunk!" I screamed as loudly as I could, but still the man did not stop. "He's not drunk. He's a retard! Okay? He's retarded!"

The minute I said the word, I understood the depth and irrevocability of my betrayal. I felt unmoored, like an astronaut floating into space. The bartender lowered Malcolm to the ground. He was crying loudly now, his mouth open, saliva stretching from one lip to the other, his sounds ugly and pathetic. Everyone in the bar was staring, and so was Laurel, who stood by the door. I knew she had heard me.

"Get these kids out of here now," the bartender growled at her.

She gathered Malcolm in her arms and held him close, patting him down as if she were trying to feel if this fresh shame had left him badly wounded. I stepped toward them, but her arms tightened around him, and I realized that she was not protecting him from the bartender but from me.

Richard stood outside the bar smoking a cigarette. Laurel, with her arm around Malcolm's shoulders, headed toward our car. I hesitated.

"We're leaving, Ares. Get in the car."

"No."

"Do what your mother says," Richard said.

"Oh, please," Laurel said. "Do not play daddy now, alright?"

"Shut the fuck up," he said under his breath.

"Get in the car, Ares. Right now."

"I want to stay with Richard."

"Hey, ho!" Richard said, surprised. "I don't remember extending the invitation."

"Please," I pleaded. "Please can I stay with you? Just for tonight?"

"Well, I don't know about that, kiddo," he said, glancing nervously at Laurel.

"I don't want to go home."

"Great," Laurel said. "That's just great."

I moved closer to Richard.

"I didn't say yes," he said. "You should go home with your mother."

"If he doesn't want to come home, I'm not going to force him," she said. "Take him. Get a taste of what you'll be missing."

"Fuck you."

"That was my first mistake."

Richard turned and headed for his Jeep. "Come if you're coming," he said. I ran and slid into the passenger seat just as he started the engine. "But you're sleeping on the floor."

"Okay."

"I'm not giving up my bed for your bad mood."

He gunned the engine. I watched as Laurel helped Malcolm into the backseat of her car. She stood in her open door.

A corona of yellow light outlined her body and her loose curls, but I couldn't see her face. I wondered if she was waiting for me to change my mind. But she shut Malcolm's door, sat down behind the wheel, and drove away. Richard put the Jeep into gear and drove so fast out of the parking lot that I had to hold on to the dashboard.

"It's like a getaway," I said.

"You never get away," he said. "You'll be dragging your sorry ass and your sorry story around with you for the rest of your life."

Instead of heading toward his trailer, he drove out of Slab City, onto the highway. He switched gears, the Jeep lurched, and we headed toward the dark outlines of the Chocolate Mountains.

"Where are we going?" I said, hugging myself against the wind.

"Just winding down. I'm not a person who can just go home and sleep. Need a little transition time."

"Me too."

"Yeah? What do you do to wind down?"

"Read, I guess."

"I drive. I tried to figure it out once. I've probably driven more than half my life."

"Where do you go?"

"Anywhere. It doesn't really matter to me."

"Where do you go when you leave here every year?"

"North. Where it's cool. I don't know how you people survive a summer here. It isn't fit for humans."

"What do you do there? In the north?"

"Depends what work there is where I end up. Depends how hungry I am."

"I can't wait until I'm old enough to drive."

"Where will you go?"

I was embarrassed to have no ready answer. As much as I'd thought about leaving, I'd never considered a destination. My life was a half-baked idea that would never turn out. "Iceland," I said, the first place that came to mind.

"Iceland?"

"Yeah."

"There's a little bit of water between you and Iceland."

"I'll have a car that turns into a boat."

"Amphibious," Richard said appreciatively. "Now you're talking."

"And it'll have a TV. And a refrigerator with anything you want to eat in it."

"Sounds like my kind of car."

I leaned my head back and closed my eyes.

When I woke up, the Jeep was parked. Richard sat beside me, smoking, squinting into the night as if it were a movie whose plot was hard to follow. The headlights of the car illuminated a hardscrabble landscape of boulders sitting complacently as gorillas, and low-lying ocotillo and cholla, their spiked tips pointing into the night like fingers. During the day, the land was a varied palette of browns but now it was just dark and darker. Five feet from where Richard parked stood a sign that read "Government Restricted Area—Keep Out." There were no fences to enforce this, which made the warning even more menacing because it was up to each individual to figure out where the boundary between safety and danger lay. I scanned the washes and gullies that gave definition to the seeming monolith of the desert, and then my eye picked out something I was not familiar with that looked like a miniature blimp planted nose first into the ground. The impact of this thing had carved a shallow, thirty-foot-wide crater into the desert floor. Just as I turned to ask Richard what it was, a sound like a train barreling down on the Jeep roared by so close I felt the vibration in my chest. The ground beneath the car shook. Lights stung the sky as planes streaked overhead. I ducked. When I straightened up, my heart beat in time with the rhythmic pulse of helicopter engines as they flew by dropping bombs onto the ground.

"Cobra," Richard yelled, pointing at a plane. "They got the Sea Knights out, too." Something exploded and pieces of metal sprayed into the air. I pointed wordlessly. "Target practice," he said. "Probably blew up an old five-ton."

The sweet, metallic scent of jet fuel made its way from my nose to my brain. One hundred yards away a tree caught fire. For a moment, it looked like a man, frozen in the act of trying to escape disaster.

"Dumping napalm." Richard shook his head. "Just some nice boys getting ready to bomb the shit out of some people they never met." He checked his watch. "They're almost done for the night." And minutes later, as if at his command, the sound and lights of the planes disappeared, and the desert sky turned dark again, illuminated now only by the discrete fires dotting the ground and the stars above, so copious it was as if Malcolm, in one of his outbursts, had shaken a paintbrush and spattered that black canvas with a million dots of white.

The silence that followed was profound, an emptiness so devoid of life that it was more terrifying to me than the bombs. It was broken by the grinding of car gears. Headlights of vehicles I hadn't even realized were parked nearby snapped on, and the cars started traveling across the terrain. They were not like cars I'd ever seen. These buggies were jerry-built affairs, stripped of hoods and windshields. The back wheels were twice the diameter of the front, so that the cars looked like donkeys kicking up their legs as they bounced over the desert floor.

"Rats coming out of their holes," Richard said.

Occasionally a car stopped and a man hopped out, grabbed something from the ground, threw it into the back of his vehicle, and drove on again.

"Got himself a bomb fin there," Richard said coolly, observing the scrapper.

"Who are these people?"

"Crazy guys," Richard said, nodding. "Used to be more of them."

"Where are they now?"

"Dead. Or busted. It's not exactly the easiest living you could think of."

"But there's stuff out there?" I said, my excitement growing. "Bombs and stuff?"

"Oh, yeah. Bomb fins, shell casings, napalm cannisters . . ."

"You could make a hundred dollars a night I bet."

Richard smiled. "Hundreds. Depending on the market."

"Let's go."

"No way, kiddo."

"Please."

"I've had my war. This is for the guys with a death wish. Some of those babies are live. They could blow your head right off. Even the inert bastards will crush you to death. Who do you think is going to win: you or a thousand pounds of metal?"

"We'll be careful."

"There's no such thing as careful. There's luck. Good and bad."

"C'mon."

"Do you understand what 'no' means?" he said, his usually quiet voice rising sharply.

But I was too enraptured by the idea of the illicit treasure hunt to pay attention to him. This adventure seemed dangerous and foolhardy. But, after what had happened at the bar, I was no longer trapped in the life of the careful, guilt-ridden boy I had once been. I felt that I could do anything. I slid from my seat and jumped to the ground and ran into the path of the Jeep's headlights. Richard yelled and swore at me, but I didn't care. I ran toward something shining on the ground. I was sure I had found a bomb. I dropped to my knees just as the ground began to shake. Lights of oncoming planes obliterated the lesser stars.

"Ares, watch out!" Richard yelled. He ran to me then grabbed me up like a hawk picking off a mouse and threw me down into a crater, falling on top of me just as the planes loosed their payloads all around us. I felt as if my body had turned inside out and my blood and bones were exposed. I thought I was dead.

We stayed like that until well after the planes had disappeared from the sky. Richard was heaving; I felt his heart beating against my back. Finally he rolled off me and stood up. "You stupid little shit!" he yelled with all the force of his pent-up rage and fear. He climbed out of the crater and headed toward the Jeep. I scrambled to keep up. The ground was littered with white nylon from parachute bombs that shifted in the small breeze like jellyfish. My foot brushed against something hard, and when I looked down, I realized I was standing next to a bomb.

"Richard?" I called weakly.

"Move it, Ares," he said, without turning back.

"I can't."

"Move your goddamn ass!"

"It's a bomb."

He stopped and turned. "Shit!" he said angrily, but when he grasped the situation, his manner changed. His voice became hushed and steady. "Okay," he said, coming close. "Do not move. Just take it easy, okay? Nothing's going to happen." When he was near me, he looked down at the bomb and sighed visibly. "See the brown stripe? It's a dummy. It's not going to hurt you." He reached out and pulled me to him.

"I'm sorry," I said, pressing myself into his body.

"You can't fuck around out here," he said.

"I'm sorry."

"Sorry's no good when you're dead."

I tightened my arms around his waist.

"You dumb shit," he said, but his anger was gone.

When we returned to the Jeep, he started the engine but didn't put the car into gear. He sat with his hands between his legs, his body bent toward the steering wheel as if he were praying. His bald head shone in the dashboard lights, and the veins above his temples throbbed. "What kind of an asshole does a thing like that?" he said to himself.

"I'm sorry."

"What kind of an asshole brings a kid to a place like this?"

DURING THE DRIVE BACK TO the Slabs, he didn't speak. Once inside the Airstream, he collected a blanket, a sheet, and one of the pillows from his bed, then laid them in the narrow space between the sink and stove and the small laminated table. "Get some sleep," he said, lying down on the floor and arranging the blanket around his body. "And don't trip over me if you need to take a piss in the middle of the night."

"I thought I didn't get the bed."

"And flick that light off by your head."

I reached up and turned off the light. It was pitch black around me. I couldn't see my hand in front of my face. "Richard?"

"What?"

"What did you do in the war?"

"Kept bugs from crawling up my asshole."

"No, really. What did you do?"

"Tried not to get killed."

"Did you kill anybody?"

"That's a dumb question."

"Do you think it's wrong to kill people in war?"

"I think if someone's trying to kill me, I'll try and kill him first. Once they start that game, you just follow the rules."

"It's a game?"

"It's action and consequence. You think beyond that, you start worrying about right and wrong, and you're dead."

He was quiet for a long time. I wondered if he had fallen asleep. Finally, he sighed deeply. "You know who comes out ahead in a war?" he said.

"Who?"

"The ones who believe in the story."

"What story?"

"The one they tell you to get you to fight. It's just like a fairy tale—bad guys, good guys. That's not the way life is. But in war, you take a flying leap into fantasyland. People who do that make it the longest."

"I don't believe in fantasies."

"Good thing you're not a soldier."

We were quiet for a time.

"Richard?"

"Go to sleep."

"Did it ever rain in Vietnam?"

"Rain?" he said, his voice slurring with tiredness. "Poured.

Your boots would fill with water. Your feet would stink like something dead."

"Do guns work when they're wet?"

"Some do. The right kind of guns do."

"But some don't?"

For a while, he said nothing. "The look on the face of a guy whose equipment fails?" he said, finally. "That's the worst kind of look."

"What does it look like?"

"Like he just saw the whole truth of everything."

The next day, he hooked the Airstream to the Jeep. He dropped me at the general store in Bombay Beach, drove back onto the highway, and headed north.

WITH RICHARD GONE, LAUREL CRAWLED up inside of herself. She became so distracted that there were times I thought she forgot about us entirely. I knew what I had said at the bar made her despise me and I vacillated between a steely pride and despair at this turn of events. In the mornings, we got ready for school and she for work in a tense quiet that was punctuated only by Malcolm's sounds. The trailer felt overcrowded as if the emotions that ran between my mother and me were extra people. When we passed each other, my muscles tightened as I tried to become small enough so that we would not touch.

When the day arrived to return to Mrs. Poole's, I was eager to go. I planned to get through my homework as quickly as possible so I could garden. I looked forward to the sharp nod of approval she would give me when she saw how well I did my job. When her front door opened, I nearly hurtled inside before I realized that the person standing in the doorway was not Mrs. Poole, but Kevin. I felt the reverse of what Laurel had instilled in me that made me never open the trailer door to strangers. I had the feeling that I had knocked on the door of someone who might hurt me.

ELEVEN

"Hey," Kevin said, as if seeing me and Malcolm was commonplace. He wore a black Styx shirt. His arms emerged from the short sleeves like pale poles. He was barefoot, and his toes were as long as French fries. His hair had grown out slightly since I had seen him last, and he looked older and more knowing. His lack of interest in me was undeniable and compelling.

"That kid is here!" he yelled as he slid back into the house and disappeared down a hallway.

Malcolm ran inside, but I didn't move from the doorway. Suddenly, the house felt forbidden. Every expectation I had of my peaceful time there and of a kind of future that had been forming in my mind in which I somehow belonged more in this house than in my own evaporated. Mrs. Poole appeared in the front hallway.

"Kevin is back," I said.

"That's right," she said, smiling uncertainly. "Don't you have homework?"

I went into the living room, sat down on my regular

chair, and opened my backpack, but I couldn't focus on work. Even though Kevin was nowhere in sight, I felt like he was watching me. At the back of the house a mystery was taking place: a door opened, a toilet flushed. I heard television laughter, and then a door closed and the sound dulled. I felt foolish sitting in the formal room, a place I knew Kevin would never choose to be. I couldn't imagine that self-possessed and incurious boy taking an interest in the books, photos, or porcelain statues that had captivated me during the past months. His presence made my love for the house seem childish.

I went and stood at the doorway between the living room and the kitchen. Mrs. Poole held Malcolm's hand to her lips as she said the word "cookie." Then she put his hand to his mouth and repeated the word. He said nothing, so she brought his hand back to her lips and started the exercise again.

"He can't talk," I said.

"Yes he can," she said, without taking her eyes off him. "There are many ways to communicate."

Malcolm reached for the cookie she had laid out on the table as a reward. She covered the cookie and shook her head. "Cookie," she repeated.

"I finished my work," I lied. "I can do the gardening now."

She sighed and turned away from Malcolm, who used the opportunity to take the cookie and stuff it into his mouth. "That's Kevin's job. We have another thirty minutes here please," she said.

I walked down the short, carpeted hallway toward the sound of the television. I ran my hand over the textured wallpaper, which was hung with paintings of forests. These were dark, secretive places so different from what I was used to, but I had the feeling these were places Mrs. Poole would have preferred to the desert that killed her vegetables and caused her to keep her shades pulled down even during the day. I heard Kevin moving in one room and I knocked lightly on his door. Just as I changed my mind and turned away, the door opened. His expression was sharp and suspicious.

"Bathroom's next door," he said.

"I don't need to go."

The air in his room was close and warm and smelled locker-room sweet.

"What do you want?" he said.

"What are you watching?"

He walked back into his room and turned off the TV. "Just some crap. What's your name again?"

"Ares."

"Oh right. Your parents are astrology freaks?"

"Not really."

"At least they didn't name you Cancer, right?" When he laughed, he looked younger than fifteen. Small dimples appeared in his cheeks, and his shoulders rose up around his ears. He seemed more like a boy my age whose body had got the better of him. He fingered items on his desk—a pen, a paperweight, a book. A bright white baseball sat inside a stiff mitt.

"Do you play baseball?" I said.

"I played baseball, you know, once, when I first got here, so they gave me this," he said, touching the mitt. "I say, you know, kites are cool, and the next day there's a new kite."

"You should say you like airplanes. Real airplanes."

Kevin's smile was slow to come, not because he didn't get the joke, but because he was deciding whether to give me the gift of his approval. "Or money," he said. "I should say I like money. Lots of it."

The room felt as carefully planned as the living room, as if each piece of furniture and decoration had been arranged by a person thinking of what a child's room should look like. A group of books stood at the back of the desk between bronze bookends shaped like horse heads. A framed map hung on one wall, a poster showing all the flags of the world on another. I recognized these types of posters from school.

"This place is almost as bad as the center," he said, following my gaze. "They won't let me go out alone."

"How come?"

"Trust is earned," he said, making quotation marks in the air.

"Are you home for good?"

He smiled at a private joke. "I guess that's up to me. That's what they say, anyway. They talk about choices like you really have any. Like, was it my choice to go to the center? Like, would you go to school if you had the choice?"

"I hate school."

"Exactly. You think it's my choice to be here?"

"You have a cool room."

"She cleans it too much. I think she looks through my stuff. You go to Niland?"

"Yeah."

"Watch your back. I was there for a while. That place is fucked up." He sat back down on his bed. "What's wrong with your brother?"

"He's kind of . . . got something wrong with his brain." I remembered Kevin swinging nimbly from ring to ring. Kevin would not have dropped a baby. "He bit a teacher at school."

Kevin's laugh was a short, unhappy bullet of sound. "She probably deserved it."

"When did you get back?"

"Two days and a million years ago. Got my learner's permit, but they took it away. They took my bike, too."

"Will you get them back?"

"Not for the probationary period," he said, making the same quote marks with his hands.

"You're on probation?"

"You ask a lot of questions."

In the kitchen, Malcolm screamed. Kevin raised his eyebrows. "She's torturing him, too," he said. Then he winced as if some invisible person had yelled at him, maybe one of the monitors from the center. "Nah," he said, reversing himself. "Everyone does the best they can."

The kitchen chairs scraped against the floor. "We come once a week," I said, quickly leaving the room.

"Lucky you," he said.

* * *

THAT NIGHT, I WOKE TO the sound of a siren outside my window. Its hollow notes disappeared as they were swallowed up by the desert. My half-awake mind stumbled from one fragment of thought to another until I was fully awake. I looked at the clock: three-fifteen. I told myself not to think about it, but the memory had already arrived and was standing at the doorway of my consciousness, holding its bags, waiting to be invited in. There was the gas station on that hot day, there was my baby brother in my arms. I tried to confuse the story by thinking about Kevin, wondering why he had hit Mrs. Poole, what she had done to make him so angry. But the story of my own crime stood stubbornly behind the other thoughts, and I surrendered. Five years later, I could still feel Malcolm's awkward weight and I reexperienced the disbelief I had felt when he lay on the ground and I did not even understand yet that he had fallen. I grunted angrily, trying to chase away my thoughts. I turned my face toward my pillow and roared again and again until my throat became raw and I started to cough. I got up and left my room.

The main room of the trailer was dark. Malcolm was asleep. The card curtain was closed, but the lamp by Laurel's bed was lit, and a soft, amber light showed through the strands.

"Baby?" her voice was thick and groggy. "Was that you coughing? Are you okay?"

"I'm just getting water."

"Let me see you."

I drew the curtain to one side. A book lay open on her chest. Curls of hair were pasted to her forehead. She inched herself up so that she was half-sitting.

"I can't sleep these days. I can't read either. I keep reading the same page over and over."

"I have to pee."

"I'm going to have a baby."

"What?"

"That's why I've been so tired and sick." She smiled, looking down at her stomach. "You guys never made me sick. But this one is giving me a run for my money, I tell you."

I felt like a hundred people were yelling inside my brain.

"How about that?" she said.

"Huh?"

"Huh?" She laughed, imitating my slow-witted response. "We're going to have a new baby to love."

"When?"

"A while yet. Early September, I think. You're going to be a big brother all over again."

"Is Richard the dad?"

Her smile disappeared. "Richard isn't part of the story anymore. He made that crystal clear."

"Is that why he went away?"

"Listen, you can spend a lifetime worrying about why things happen and in the end it doesn't make a difference. All that matters is what you do next. And we're going to have a baby."

"I don't want one."

"What are you talking about?"

She said something else, but I couldn't hear her. My body was flooding with adrenaline. The sound in my head grew louder. I had to shout to be heard over it. "Why do all the dads in this family leave?"

"Keep your voice down!"

"What do you do to them?"

"We don't need a dad," she hissed. "We're fine."

"We're fine?" A sharp, hysterical laugh escaped from my throat.

Her mouth fell open as if I had slapped her. "A baby will be good for Malcolm," she said. "It's good to have someone to take care of. It was good for you."

"Good for me?" The obviousness of her lie enraged me. "I hate you!" I said it again, mesmerized by the power of the words. Her face crumbled as if it were made of dry clay. I dropped the curtain. I grabbed my pants and shoes from my room and went to the front door.

"Ares!" she called from behind her curtain. "Come back here. Right now!"

Malcolm stirred on his couch.

"You woke him up!" I yelled loudly enough to ensure my claim would be true. "And it's your fault this time."

It was still dark when I arrived at Mrs. Poole's. A ring of lights around the perimeter of the house made it appear to be floating on a black sea. Mr. Poole's truck was parked in the driveway next to her car. Whatever idea I'd had about coming here, whatever escape or solace I was looking for disinte-

grated when I saw the two cars side by side. Now that Kevin
was home, the Pooles were a family that had closed ranks. I
was about to remount my bike when I noticed a pile of plants
and grasses lying by the edge of the vegetable garden. I knelt
down. In among the weeds and rocks were green broom and
buckwheat, the viruses Mrs. Poole wanted to eradicate. But a
bean plant had been pulled out of the ground, too, its roots
still intact. I sorted through the pile more carefully and
found two more young shoots Kevin had mistaken for weeds.
I separated them from the pile, lifting them carefully, making
sure to support their delicate stems.

"What are you stealing?"

Kevin stood in a spill of light. He wore a T-shirt and wrinkled boxer shorts. His face was creased from sleep.

"I wasn't taking anything."

"What are you fucking doing?" His legs were muscular
and hairy—a man's legs.

"I was just . . . some of these are good. Like this." I held
up the bean plant. "You can replant it. She won't know."

"So, you're the gardener or something?"

"No."

"You just go to other people's houses in the middle of the
night and steal their shit?"

"It's not like that," I said weakly, but I couldn't say what
it was, either. I felt like I had woken out of a dream that was
fleeing from my mind just as I was about to remember what
the point of it was.

"Maybe I ought to get one of them out here," he said,
cocking his head toward the house.

"No. Please."

A smile leaked across his face. "I'm not a snitch. I mean, if you get off doing other people's work, I'm not gonna stop you. I hate this shit."

"I can do it for you. I don't mind."

He considered the offer. "Maybe. Only she can't find out. She's all about chores. Taking responsibility. Pulling your weight. Weeding is supposed to be part of my re-ha-bil-i-ta-tion." He tore apart the word. In the spaces between syllables resided a whole history of Kevin I had no access to, but that I wanted to know. "What's that one?" he said, pointing to the plant in my hand.

"Bean. This one's burro brush," I said, picking up another plant. "She doesn't like it, but it will flower."

He twisted his mouth in a not entirely generous appraisal. "So, you're a plant freak?"

"I did the gardening when you were gone." I was about to tell him that I got paid for the job but thought the better of the laughable two dollars. "She lent me a plant book."

"Yeah. She's all about books. 'Look it up in a book,' " he said, imitating her. "Like she knows the answer but makes you look it up anyway."

"Well, your mom's a librarian."

"Foster mom. It's a temporary thing."

"You're going to leave?"

"They kicked me out before. Sent me to the center. You know they make money off me? Fostering's, you know, a profit situation. That's why they took me back after I served my time. They need the dough."

"She said it wasn't a prison."

"Ha! Maybe she should spend three fucking months in there!"

"If you leave here where will you go?"

"Some other family that takes in strays. I age out when I'm eighteen. That will be freedom, man. Get me out of this system."

"What will you do?"

"Everything. Anything. Go to Alaska. Yeah," he said, as if he had just thought of the idea and liked the sound of it. "I'm going to go to Alaska. Meet some Eskimos."

"How many places have you lived?"

"She's my eighth placement."

"Mrs. Poole?"

"It's funny the way you call her that. Like you're at school."

"I heard you robbed a store."

"I didn't rob any stores," he said, his lip curling at the insult. "If I'd have robbed a store, I wouldn't have got caught."

"That's what some kids said."

"They're wrong."

"Did you really hit her?"

"Yeah."

"Why?"

He looked away, shifting uncomfortably.

"I don't know. I just did."

"So she sent you to that place?"

"*He* did." He stared at me for a long moment.

The screen door at the back of the house whined as it opened.

"Shit," Kevin said. He took the bean plant from me. "Get out of here."

But it was too late. Mrs. Poole stepped around the side of the house. "Ares?" she said. She held her bathrobe closed at her neck. "What are you doing here? It's the middle of the night."

"I was just riding around," I mumbled, lifting my bike off the ground.

"Kevin?" Mrs. Poole said accusingly.

"Hey," Kevin said, "I just heard something. I thought it was a thief. Then I come out here and see this kid messing around in the garden. And then he pulls up this bean plant. And I'm, you know, hey, that's a good plant."

Mrs. Poole took the plant from him like it was an injured child he might harm further. She looked at me suspiciously. I wanted to tell her the truth, but a look from Kevin told me to say nothing.

"I'll call your mother to come get you," she said. "She's probably worried sick."

"No! Don't call. Please. I can ride home."

"It's not safe. And if your mother gets angry, as she should, that's your consequence."

"She doesn't feel well right now. She's really sick. She's having a baby."

Mrs. Poole was taken aback. "Another baby?"

"In September."

She took a moment to consider. "Alright. I'll wake Jerry,

and he will take you." She turned to go inside. "Let's go, Kevin," she said.

"I'll stay out here. Make sure he doesn't pull up any more of our vegetables."

"Kevin. Inside. Right now."

Kevin flashed a grin I knew had nothing to do with happiness.

A few minutes later, Mr. Poole came out of the front door pulling a jacket over his shirt, followed by Kevin. Mrs. Poole stood in the doorway.

"He should stay here," she said.

"It'll just be a half hour," Mr. Poole said.

"It's a school night, Jerry. He needs his sleep. I'll be fine."

"You are not staying alone with him," Mr. Poole said firmly, putting a hand on Kevin's back and guiding him to the truck.

I sat in the cab between Mr. Poole and Kevin. A laminated security pass dangled from the rearview mirror. "You're a park ranger?" I said, recognizing the symbol on the badge.

"I work for the department. I'm a biologist."

"Oh."

"You sound disappointed."

"I thought you were a cop."

"Ha!" Kevin yelped.

"Why would you think that?" Mr. Poole said.

"I don't know," I said, not wanting to admit I'd been studying the photos in Mrs. Poole's house, imagining their whole life.

"I'm not the police," he said. "But I do keep those pelicans in line."

"My brother likes pelicans," I said. "He likes birds."

"Then he and I have something in common."

"He wishes he was a bird."

"Yeah, well, don't we all," Mr. Poole said.

"I don't want to be any kind of bird," Kevin mumbled.

"You're already a weird bird," Mr. Poole said, smiling slyly.

Something eased between them.

"You've made that joke a hundred times," Kevin said.

"And it's always funny."

"It's not funny. That's the thing you don't get. It was never funny." But Kevin couldn't hide his smile.

"Ares here thought it was funny. Right, Ares?"

"Well," I said, uncomfortably.

"Now you're in a tight spot," Mr. Poole said lightly. "Which one of us are you going to insult?"

"I thought it was sort of funny," I said.

Kevin laughed loudly. "Chicken shit!"

"Okay Kevin. Settle down."

"Bawk . . . bawk, bawk, bawk," Kevin said.

"Kevin!" Mr. Poole said harshly. "That's enough!"

Kevin stared at his hands, his jaw working.

We drove in silence. "Let's have some tunes," Mr. Poole said finally. "Find something good, Kevin."

Kevin reached across me. The radio touched down lightly on a variety of stations and static as he searched.

"There," Mr. Poole said. "That's good."

Kevin homed in on the station, and "Surfer Girl" emerged through the debris of static.

"We saw those guys once," Mr. Poole said. "We were living in Vermont. Went all the way to Boston to see them."

"You and Mrs. Poole?" I asked. I didn't know what Vermont looked like but I thought it might be full of forests like the ones pictured in the paintings in their home. Maybe a place like that was her natural habitat.

Mr. Poole nodded. "Drove down and back in one day. We ended up pulling over and sleeping in the car. That's when we were young and stupid."

Mr. Poole glanced at Kevin. Kevin looked down at his lap, trying to suppress a smile. Mr. Poole grinned. "Go ahead," he said. "Say it. I know you want to."

"Now you're old and stupid!" Kevin said.

"He's been using that line ever since he came to us."

We passed the gas station which was lit up even at that late hour. A man stood by one of the pumps. I recognized him—it was Ronald Epps, the brother of Calvin, one of the boys who had beaten me up. He was a drug dealer, and I imagined he was out this late doing business. As we drove past, he watched us, his eyes narrowing as if he were trying to draw a bead.

"Fuck," Kevin mumbled as he slid down in his seat and covered his face with his hand.

"Is there a problem, Kevin?" Mr. Poole said.

"No."

"Let's clean up the language."

"Sorry."

We turned off the highway at the sign for Bombay Beach. Kevin looked quickly over his shoulder and seemed to relax. He stared out the window at the passing trailers, some lying in darkness, some lit by harsh floods. A few dogs barked, throwing themselves at fences or pulling against chains. Kevin's hand found his chin, where he rubbed his finger over the growth there. "You live here?"

"It's at the end of this street," I said, pointing. Our trailer looked forlorn, with nothing to decorate it other than the randomly lit Christmas bulbs Laurel had not taken down. We didn't have a yard or an outdoor furniture set. We had no garden. Kevin looked at me as if reconsidering an opinion he had formed. Mr. Poole got out of the truck.

"You have a purple front door," Kevin said. I heard the bike scrape against the truck bed.

"My mom painted it. She kind of takes old things and fixes them up."

"Is that her job?"

"She gives massages."

"Yeah? Does she give you a hand job if you tip extra?"

"No!"

Kevin smiled at me. "Man, take a joke! I was just kidding."

I slid across the seat toward the door. He grabbed my arm to stop me.

"Thanks for covering for me with the plants. That was cool."

"Okay."

"I didn't mean that shit I said about you being chicken. I say a lot of shit I don't mean. I don't know why."

Mr. Poole appeared at the open car door with my bike. He watched as I got out of the car, took the bike and leaned it against the trailer. I climbed the steps to our door. "I'm okay," I said, turning back, wishing they would leave.

"I'll wait to make sure someone's home," Mr. Poole said.

"She's probably sleeping."

"I'll wait."

I opened the door and gave Mr. Poole a thumbs up. He looked uncertain but finally climbed into his truck and drove away.

The trailer was dark, but as I walked past Malcolm's couch I saw that Laurel was lying next to him. Her eyes glittered in the dark.

"Where were you?" she said softly.

"Nowhere."

"Who was that outside?"

"Nobody."

"I was about to call the police."

"I'm fine."

"You're twelve years old."

"So?"

"So you don't walk out of here in the middle of the night."

"I can do whatever I want."

"No, you can't."

"Are you going to ground me?"

"What's happened to you?"

"What do you mean?"

"You used to be so . . . nice."

"I thought you didn't like nice people. I thought you said nice people were stupid. Like your parents."

"I need you to be okay with this baby. I can't do it without you." She waited for my response but I said nothing. She put a protective arm across Malcolm's chest. "Shhh," she whispered, more to herself than him, as though she were quieting voices in her own head.

"I'M GONNA BLOW," KEVIN SAID, pacing his room from one end to the other. Three weeks had passed, and I had begun to spend my time during Malcolm's sessions in Kevin's room. I could tell Mrs. Poole didn't like this. She kept reminding me about my homework, but she never stopped me. She was careful around Kevin, and whenever she told him to do things for her—take out the garbage, or make his bed—she seemed hesitant and she chose her words as though she thought the wrong ones might trigger something dangerous. Kevin ruled the house with his dismissive grunts and withering expressions.

"At least at the center, I had people to talk to," he continued. "I had things to *do. Fuck.* I am so fucking bored. I don't know why she brought me back here. It's like a fucking prison. My other placements were ten times better than this."

"Where were you before?" I said. I could hear Malcolm's inside-out laughter coming from the kitchen.

"When they brought me here the first time, I was twelve," he said, ignoring my question. "I had to play catch with Jerry for, like, five hours. I mean, it was torture, man. And all the time she's asking me these questions. What do I like to do? What do I like to eat? What's my favorite book? I thought if I missed the ball, they wouldn't take me, but it was hard to concentrate because she wouldn't shut up. And, you know, I didn't want to go back to that group home I was in before. They had staff that went around at night because some of those kids were so messed up they'd fuck with you in your sleep. It never happened to me, but I've seen it, man. With my own eyes. Eight-year-old rapists. When I got placed out I was, you know, I don't care who you are. Just take me out of this hellhole. The first night I came here, we went to a ball game."

"That's cool."

"No, because, you know, the whole time, I'm thinking about what my case worker said, that I better be on my best behavior, because, you know, I'm too old to be cute, and maybe this is my last chance. People don't want big kids 'cause they're too fucked up and there's nothing you can do about it. So I can't even dig the game, you know, yell and stuff, because I'm thinking, maybe I'll swear by mistake, or maybe they don't want a kid who yells at sports. You know, like, in all the places I've been, everybody just wants you to shut up and not cause any problems and act normal even if they are freaks. I've been with some freaky people, man. People with no business taking kids like me. Like *I* got problems? *They're* the ones with problems."

"Why doesn't Mrs. Poole have her own kids?"

"Her equipment must be broken. Maybe someone was trying to tell her something." He cackled.

"Is your real mother dead?"

"No!" he said, as if offended by the suggestion.

"Why don't you live with her?"

He shrugged but his expression was strange. It wandered around his face, searching out someplace safe to settle. "You got to get me out of here," he said urgently. He grabbed me by the shoulders so our faces were inches apart. I could smell his breath. "I've got people I need to see."

"Who?"

"You gotta help me."

"I can't."

He let me go. "All I need is a fucking car," he said to himself. "A fucking bicycle even."

"I have a bike."

"You do?"

"The one I ride out here."

"Oh, right. That one." He said it as though he'd never noticed how Malcolm and I arrived at his house, week after week. "Yeah, but that's *your* bike. What good does that do me?"

I couldn't stop myself. "You could borrow it."

"Really? Are you sure? Because that would be amazing."

"I guess."

"You could ride it out here tonight, and then I'll take it and go do my business."

I was disappointed. I had imagined we would go for a ride

together, maybe out to Slab City. He could pedal and I could ride on the handlebars. I would show him where Richard took us scrapping. If we found anything, I'd let Kevin keep it. "What am I supposed to do while you're gone?"

"You know, just hang out."

"Here?"

"Exactly!" he said, as if I had come up with this brilliant solution myself. "They won't notice. They go to bed old-people-early." He clapped his hands together. "So tonight. Okay? Just ride up around the back of the house to my window. I'll be waiting."

The door opened. Mrs. Poole stood with her hand on the knob. "Time to go, Ares," she said.

I looked at Kevin, hoping he would laugh or indicate in some way that this was all a joke. But he threw his arm around me.

"This kid's cool," he said. "He's gonna be my cool little brother."

"I'm glad you're getting along," she said warily.

Kevin punched me playfully on the shoulder and pushed me gently toward the door. When I looked back at him, he winked, and all my worries about the bike disintegrated. Until that moment, I had not realized how lonely I was, and how it had been impossible for me to imagine friendship. I was mesmerized by Kevin.

At the front door Mrs. Poole handed me a large manila envelope. "Give this to your mother," she said. "I want her to look at these brochures. It's very important. I did some research."

"Okay."

Malcolm slipped out the door. When I turned to follow, Mrs. Poole put a hand on my shoulder. "She doesn't look at the papers I send home, does she."

"She's busy."

"I don't understand. Doesn't she want to help him?"

The intimacy of her comment, and the way she assumed I would share in her judgment of my mother, startled me. But I did not defend Laurel. "Should I tell her Malcolm did good today?"

"Did *well*," she said, but there was no steam behind her correction.

THAT NIGHT, LAUREL LEFT ME to clean up after dinner while she went to her room to lie down. Malcolm smelled like old food, so I took him to the bathroom. He submitted to being undressed without much fuss, but once in the tub, he splashed water all over the floor, the walls, and me.

"Cut it out," I hissed, not wanting Laurel to hear, but when Malcolm didn't calm down, I grabbed his wrists. "Stop it! Stop it!" I whispered. He started to kick, and water sloshed over the lip of the tub. I squeezed his wrists tighter and I felt what those boys must have felt when they threw rocks at him: the savage pleasure of hurting someone who was weak. He looked at me not with an expression of pain but of confusion, as if he didn't understand why I wanted to harm him. I dropped his hands, frightened by how easily I could destroy him and how good it would make me feel.

Once I was sure that Laurel and Malcolm were both asleep, I rode my bike through the dark streets of Bombay Beach and onto the highway. Occasionally a car or truck passed, nearly pushing my bike off the road in its gust of wind. I pedaled faster then, trying to take advantage of the path described by the headlights. When I reached Mrs. Poole's house, I left my bike by the curb so that the wheels wouldn't make noise as I crossed the gravel driveway. At the back of the house, Kevin's window glowed softly behind gauzy white curtains. I picked up a handful of gravel from the decorative border that circled the house and gently tossed the rocks at the window. The room went dark, the window opened, and Kevin's sneaker, then leg appeared, followed by the rest of his body.

"Where's the bike?" he whispered, as he noiselessly lowered himself onto the ground.

"I left it on the street," I said, humiliated by his disregard for my bravery. I followed as he ran to the front of the house, then stopped to watch as he sprinted across the front yard and mounted the bike. He pumped hard, gained speed, and coasted down the dark road.

I started toward the porch, but halfway there, I realized how exposed I was. If Mr. or Mrs. Poole were to look out the window they would see me plainly. The only safe place to hide was on the windowless side of the house near the vegetable garden. There, I slid down onto the cold ground. I didn't know what to do with myself. I tossed gravel from one hand to the next. I retied my shoes. I stared out at the vacant night until I became chilled. I drew the sleeves of my sweater over my hands, pulled my knees to my chest, and ducked my head between them. The close air inside the pocket I'd created for my face made me drowsy. I closed my eyes and slept.

"Wake up, man. This isn't your bedroom."

I looked up to see Kevin standing above me. His eyes were red, his pupils tiny dots of black. He couldn't keep still and kept checking over his shoulder as if he thought someone were following him.

"What time is it?" I said, struggling to stand.

He held a silencing finger to his lips. "I brought you something," he whispered, handing me a folded slice of pizza. "Payment for services."

As I took the pizza, he ran silently around to the back of the house. I followed him just in time to see his legs disappear though the open window.

FOR THE NEXT TWO WEEKS, whenever I could get out of my house at night, I did. Kevin brought me all sorts of small tokens: burgers, tacos, a pack of chewing gum, an old Spider-Man comic book that was missing a cover. Each night he came back hopped up, red-eyed, and restless, but sometimes he would sit down next to me and we would talk. He showed me how to find Orion in the sky, told me that if I was ever jumped I should start acting crazy because even criminals were scared of crazy people. He showed me how to make a quarter roll across my knuckles without using my other hand. He'd learned some card tricks at the center and said he would teach them to me if I brought him a deck. He showed me how to do the Hustle, and when we both started laughing at his moves, a light came on in the house. When the light went off, and we were safe, we laughed into our shirts to muffle our sound. One night, he fished a crushed pack of cigarettes from the pocket of his jeans and I smoked my first one. He was patient as he taught me how to inhale and let go of the smoke without stinging my eyes. He called me "little brother."

TWELVE

A few weeks later, Malcolm and I arrived home from school to find Richard leaning against the side of his Jeep. He wore his cowboy hat and a camouflage vest studded with pockets. Malcolm surprised me by acknowledging Richard immediately. He made whooping sounds and started to jump.

"Whoa, boy," Richard said. "That's quite a greeting." He reached into one of the pockets of his vest, took out a seashell, and handed it to Malcolm. "Got that on the coast of Oregon."

"What are you doing here?" I said.

"Hello to you, too," he said, wrapping Malcolm in a hug. "Door's locked." He tilted his head toward the trailer.

"We lock our door."

"Any more dead bodies popping up around here?"

I drew out my key from under my shirt, where it hung on a leather thong around my neck.

"Keys to the kingdom," he said.

"Does she know you're back?"

"Thought I'd surprise her."

"She doesn't like surprises."

"Listen, man. You can give me all the hard time you want. I left. I blew it. It was a shitty thing."

Inside, he sat at the kitchen table. I took a Mountain Dew from the refrigerator and opened it.

"I'll take one of those," he said. I gave him a can and he took a long drink from it. "Looks like we're going to have one more little monster around here."

"She said you were out of the picture."

He squinted into the dark opening of the can. "I guess I deserve that."

"When she comes home, I'll tell her you're at the Slabs."

Richard shook his head. "Sold my trailer. For about half of what it was worth, which pisses me off."

"Where are you going to live?"

"I thought I'd try living here with you guys."

"Here?"

"Are you being dumb on purpose?"

By the time Laurel came home from work, Richard, Malcolm, and I were at the table, eating the spaghetti Richard had prepared. The material of her spa uniform strained over her belly. "What are you doing here?" she said.

He laughed. "This family has a way with hellos." His eyes traveled to her stomach, taking in the new geography there.

"He sold his trailer," I said.

"You shouldn't have done that," she said.

He stood and walked to her. "I'm here to give it a shot, okay? Like you said."

"Don't pin it on me," she said. "If you blame me for coming back, you'll blame me when you leave again."

"I never blame anyone else for my mistakes." He reached out and spread his hand over her stomach. He leaned close and whispered something into her hair. She smiled as he kissed her cheek.

"Get off," she said, pushing him away, but there was flirtation in her voice and in the way she brushed her body against his as she passed him on her way to set down her purse. "You made dinner," she said.

"I had some help from my friends here. Ares here is wicked with a can opener."

Laurel laid her hand on Malcolm's head. He looked up at her, his mouth opening to reveal the half-chewed food inside. "Hi, my sweet boy," she said softly. She touched my shoulder. "How was school?"

"Fine."

"Fine," she repeated for Richard's benefit. "That's all I get."

"He's a boy," Richard said.

"Is that what boys are like?" She smiled coyly. "Tell you nothing? Take everything?"

"Every last one of them."

That night I slept on her bed behind the card curtain. I was amazed by how quickly arrangements had been made, space rearranged, new teams formed. I tried to think of Laurel's room as mine, but it was still filled with her things: an Indian print scarf draped over the lamp, pots of creams crowding her bedside table. Her sheets were suffused with the perfume of her body. I heard the low rumble of Richard's voice coming from inside my old room and the warm response of Laurel's laugh. I did not sleep.

The following day, Richard drove Malcolm and me to school. "Door to door service," he said as he pulled into the parking lot.

"Are you going to do this every day?" I said.

"You'd rather take the bus?"

"We ride our bikes. Kids on the bus make fun of Mal."

"Kids can be assholes."

"I think Malcolm knows it, too."

"I'm sure he does." He looked in the rearview mirror at Malcolm.

"Mom doesn't do anything about it."

"Listen, Ares. It's not going to work out here if I get in your mother's way. I'm not here to fight any battles for you." He stared at the school building. "Why do they have to make these places so damn ugly?" he said.

A girl from my grade passed and stared into the Jeep, then looked away.

"Who's that?"

"Just some girl."

"Just some girl," he said, smiling. "Don't be an asshole to girls."

"I'm not an asshole."

"That 'some girl' has a name."

"Danielle, I guess."

"Alright then. That's what I'm talking about."

"Are you going to be like this now?"

"Like what?"

"Teaching me things? Acting like you're some kind of dad or something?"

"You got a little attitude on since I saw you last. How old are you now? Eleven?"

"Thirteen in a month!"

"Thirteen. Shit," Richard sighed, as if suddenly overwhelmed by the immensity of what he had undertaken.

I couldn't concentrate at school. Richard's arrival, and the way the family had reformed around the impending arrival of another baby, and the unspoken tension between me and my mother, all combined to make me feel that I had been pushed out of my life. Richard picked us up after school, but as soon as I got home I rode my bike to the gas station. I wanted to punch someone or hit something, find some way to release what was twisted up inside me. I put air in my tires, then went into the convenience store. The woman behind the counter talked to another customer as she worked the register. Her flame-colored fingernails were so long that she had to hold her hands awkwardly to press the keys. The *tap-tap* of her nails on the countertop as she waited for payment bored into my brain. I pretended to consider buying a bag of chips then left the store. On my way home, I stopped my bike by the side of the road, reached down the front of my jeans, and took out the pack of cards I'd stolen.

A few nights later, I crawled out of the window in my new room and brought the cards to Kevin. When he returned from wherever it was he went, he showed me the card tricks he had learned. He made my card appear at the top of the deck even though I had buried it deep within the middle.

"Show me how," I pleaded.

"Nope."

"Come on."

"No way."

I lunged for him, knocking him over. We rolled around together as the cards spluttered from his hands, me demanding that he tell me the trick, him laughing and shaking his head vigorously. Finally, I gave up and lay back on the ground, breathless.

"You're a tough little mother, you know that?" Kevin said, standing up and grinning down at me. "I don't want to get on your bad side."

"I'm baaaad," I said, raising my hands and pretending to shoot him.

He put his hand to his heart. "You got me," he said. He leaned precariously to the side, then took off around the house.

LATER THAT WEEK, RICHARD TOOK me to the hardware store so he could buy material to fix the leaking bathroom faucet. While he searched the aisles for washers and caulking, I pinched a box of nails. At the drug store a few days later, I slipped a pack of gum into my pocket. I stole a small bag of fancy dates from the shop at the date farm, and when I was paying for my milkshake, I stole a key ring shaped like a palm tree. The next day, I stole a Snickers bar from the grocery store as Laurel, Malcolm, and I squeezed through the checkout line. The woman at the register looked at me suspiciously but said nothing. My heart beat fast as we walked out of the automatic doors. I expected an alarm to go off, or for the checkout lady to call me back and have me arrested. But nothing happened. In the parking lot, Malcolm steered the cart toward the wrong car until Laurel managed to stop him. Quietly, she negotiated with him as she redirected the cart. I watched them as if they were strangers. The candy bar sat lodged in my pocket like a gun. I was a thief, and no one knew. No one understood who I really was or what I was capable of doing. Somebody looking at me would think I was just a boy with a pregnant mother. He might think I was generously helping her load the bags into the back of the car because I was good. He might admire my patience as I buckled my spastic brother into his seat. He would be wrong.

That night, I lay in bed listening to the sounds Laurel and Richard made in their bedroom. The fact that they were having sex disgusted and aroused me. Later, Richard came out of the bedroom. I heard the heavy stream of his piss hit the toilet, the gargle and swallow of the flush. The motor on the refrigerator belched as he opened its door. A bottle top clattered across the counter then bounced into the sink. Laurel began to say something, but her words got lost as he closed their door.

I kept a paper bag beneath my bed. Inside lay the pack of cards, the nails, the key ring, and all the other things I'd stolen. Each night, I stared at these things with detachment.

The small rush I'd felt stealing them had faded and could only be replaced by another theft.

"WHY AREN'T YOU EATING?" LAUREL said one night. In recent weeks, she had begun to eat with such aggressive determination that I could barely stand to look at her. Even Richard made jokes about her appetite. She put a forkful of food into her mouth, scraped it off with her teeth, then chewed, her lips rolling in and out like a cow.

"I'm not hungry."

"You should eat." She reached for another slice of bread. Richard held the plate out for her.

"You're a skinny one, Ares," Richard agreed. "We need to put some meat on you."

"I'm not the one who's pregnant," I said.

"Just looking out for my baby," Laurel said.

"Our baby," Richard said.

"Don't call me a baby," I said.

"I'm talking about this baby," she said, patting her belly. I snorted.

"I guess this is what they call adolescence," she said, rolling her eyes at Richard.

"You act like I'm a joke," I wailed.

"No we don't," she said, smiling slyly at Richard. "Richard, tell him we don't think he's a joke."

"He's dead serious as far as I'm concerned," he said.

"See?" I said.

"No. I'm sorry," she said, trying to control her laughter.

"I'm not some statistic."

"You're right, baby." She grabbed a tangerine from the bowl in the middle of the table, bit into the skin, and sucked out the juice, some of which spilled over her chin.

"Mom! You're disgusting!"

Richard's smile dropped and he grabbed my arm. "Do not talk to your mother that way, you hear?" he said.

I looked at Laurel, but she said nothing in my defense.

"Do you hear me?" he said.

"Yes."

He let go of my arm. "There's something called respect. Go to your room."

"What?" I was stunned. Laurel had never sent me to my room before. "I don't have a room."

"Don't be smart."

"Do what he says, Ares," Laurel said.

I spent two minutes in my room, then slid open the window and climbed out.

I rode to the general store and wandered down an aisle filled with cans of beans and precooked spaghetti, bags of rice and pasta. I walked up the next aisle, where the soft white bread loaves that sat at the bottom of the stacks were finally, at this late hour, exposed. They looked like fighters at the end of a losing round.

"How much?" I asked Ed, the big-chested owner of the store who stood behind the counter.

"Like it says on the price sticker."

"But it's mushed up." I showed him the loaf.

"It's still bread."

"It's for my mom."

"You want it?" Ed said as the phone rang.

"My mom says to get day-old bread because it's cheaper."

"Then you have to wait until tomorrow." He moved away from the register to answer the phone. I put two dollars on the counter. I didn't wait for the change.

Once I had ridden onto the highway, I stopped. I lifted up my shirt. I was sweating so much that I had to peel the *Playboy* I had stolen from the rack below the register off my stomach. On the cover, two naked women held pink satin over their breasts. They were sisters. I ripped open the bag of bread, took out two slices, and tossed the rest of the loaf by the side of the road.

A half hour later, I threw a pebble at Kevin's window. When he climbed out, I handed him the magazine.

"Nice going," he said, running his eyes appreciatively over the cover and taking a cursory look at the centerfold before throwing the magazine back inside his room and taking off around the corner of the house. I sat on the gravel and waited for his return. As usual, he came back jittery and glassy-eyed. He handed me a can of Coke and climbed back through his window. He held up the magazine and gave me a thumbs up. I rode back home, wishing I had not gotten rid of the rest of the loaf of bread. But there was something about my hunger, the emptiness of my body, and the exhilaration I felt having succeeded in my biggest theft yet that made me feel fast and light, like I could hover above the life around me and not be part of it.

THIRTEEN

Laurel put Richard in charge of Saturdays. Even though I argued loudly against being babysat, he made me and Malcolm accompany him to his new job maintaining the wind turbines for the power station. Despite my resistance, standing in the field of turbines gave me the same thrill I felt when I watched a marching band go through its choreographed paces. The rows of converters were neat and intentional as the rows in a strawberry field. The tall stalks gleamed an improbable white in the dusty brown landscape. Malcolm and I watched as Richard climbed the shaft of one turbine, his tool belt hanging low on one thigh, weighted down by wrenches and screwdrivers. He inched his safety strap up the metal rungs as he slowly rose higher. When he first got the job, he told us the requirements were having no fear of heights and being willing to work for next to nothing. He said lots of Indians worked the job because they had the best balance of any people on earth. I placed a hand on the second rung of the ladder and hoisted myself up.

"Get your ass down! Now!" Richard yelled, and I dropped to the ground.

Malcolm wandered down a row of the tall windmills, slapping his hand against each shaft as he passed. Richard reached the top of the ladder and balanced near the pinwheel arms of the turbine. He leaned out, anchored by his safety harness. I imagined what would happen if the harness broke and he fell. I could see his long body wheeling through the air, hammers and wrenches and screw guns fleeing, putting distance between themselves and the disaster. This was not the first time I had fantasized about disaster. The night before, Malcolm and I were watching *Happy Days*. Malcolm sat on his heels, his usual two feet from the television, while I lay on the couch behind him imagining what it would be like to put my hands around his neck and squeeze and squeeze.

Richard descended the ladder, the hollow stalk resounding with his movement. "Finito," he said, jumping down from the third rung and landing beside me. "Where's your brother?"

The land spread out from where we stood like the page of a book, and Malcolm was nowhere to be seen.

"Aw shit, Ares," Richard said. "All you had to do was keep an eye on him. Is that too damn much to ask?"

As he called Malcolm's name, I took off down a row of turbines. I knew Richard had seen into my thoughts, knew that I had wished him and my brother dead. I felt sure that if he caught me he would kill me. I ran along one row after another, trying to lose myself, but it was impossible to disappear. The turbines were too uniform, the land between them barren. Anything alien stood out like a shout.

"Ares! Boy! What the hell?" Richard called as he ran toward me, letting his tool belt drop to the ground. I crouched down and covered my head with my hands, waiting for the worst.

"Jesus Christ," Richard wheezed. "What the hell's going on?"

I peered through the triangle of my arms. He leaned over, hands on knees, catching his breath. Malcolm wandered up in back of him. I lowered my hands.

"He was just by the Jeep," he said, standing up. "He was just grabbing some shade. Why'd you have to go off like that? Nearly killed me."

THAT EVENING, LAUREL AND RICHARD were in a playful mood. He put on a Fleetwood Mac album and danced around as she prepared dinner. He moved like a tall robot, his elbows jutting out, his hands slicing air like he was doing karate. Malcolm hopped around the room.

"C'mon Ares," Richard shouted over the music. "Let's see your moves." He turned to Laurel. "Honey, time to teach your boy to dance."

Laurel smiled, dried her hands with a dishtowel, and moved toward me. When I realized what was happening, I backed up against the wall, holding out my arms to keep her away. She started to sway, her stomach riding comfortably in front of her like a ship cresting the swells of the sea. "Come on, baby. Dance with your big fat mama," she said, holding out her hands. I was horrified as I reached for her. She swung us left and right, moving nimbly despite her girth.

"Move your feet, man," Richard said. "It's called dancing."

His voice made me self-conscious. "Let go," I said, dropping her hands and jamming my own into the pockets of my jeans. Laurel cocked her head and pouted but was quickly swept up by Richard, who spun her away from me. She looked into his eyes, smiling as his hand traveled up and down her back and over her ass.

I went into what was now officially their room and closed the door. Richard's belongings occupied the top of my old dresser—his beat-up cowboy hat, a can of deodorant, a hard glasses case, a few crumpled dollar bills. One of his shirts claimed the back of my wooden desk chair. I slid open the top dresser drawer. Nestled among Laurel's underwear and bras sat her woven jewelry basket. I poured the earrings and necklaces out onto the bed. I fingered a chunk of turquoise that hung from a red silk cord, a feathered earring, a necklace I'd made in kindergarten out of gum wrappers. Something caught the light, and I moved things aside and found a gold cross I'd never seen her wear. I imagined it must have been something from her childhood, maybe something her parents had given her. I was surprised she'd kept a cross, and the new, hateful voice inside me called her a hypocrite. I heard her throaty laugh close to the door. I put the jewelry back into the basket quickly and replaced the basket in the drawer, arranging the underwear around it so it looked as though it was never moved.

* * *

WHEN I SAW KEVIN THE next week, he told me he
needed money. "She used to give me allowance. But that's a
'pri-vil-ege,'" he said. He lay on his bed staring at the ceiling. I stood nearby, tossing the baseball and catching it in the
stiff glove.

"I don't have any money," I said, the lie clanging like a
warning bell. I had saved all the money I had ever gotten—
birthday money, Christmas money, the money I'd made
weeding Mrs. Poole's garden.

Kevin clicked his tongue on the roof of his mouth dismissively.

"Why should I give you my money?" I said.

"Why should I let you hang around with me?"

"Who else do you have to hang around with?"

He sat up and snatched the ball out of the air.

"You want to play catch?" I said.

"No, I don't want to play catch," he said. "I want a fucking cigarette. Get me a smoke, man."

"Abracadabra," I waved my hands in the air. I held out
my open palm and offered him the imaginary cigarette.

"I'm not kidding, little brother," he said. "Make yourself
useful. Do you know what this is like? Do you have any
idea? I go to school. I come home. I go to school. I come
home. They watch me like a hawk. Especially him."

"Maybe your real mom will come and get you soon."

"My real mom is a strung-out bitch. She probably doesn't
even remember I exist."

"What's her name?"

"Why do you want to know?"

" 'Cause I want to know."

"Regina."

"Regina," I repeated. Then I started to laugh.

"What's so funny?"

"It's a funny name. Regina. Re-geen-a."

"It's not funny," Kevin said, but he was suppressing his smile.

"Words sound funny when you slow them down."

"What's your mother's name?"

"Laurel."

"Lore-el," he said, drawing out the syllables until they were Silly Putty in his mouth. "Lor-el. Whore-el."

"Reg-eye-nah. Va-gi-na."

"Mo-ther."

"Fuck-er."

"Mother fucker."

"Mother fucker," I said. "Mother fucker, mother fucker, mother fucker."

"Have you ever?"

"What?"

"Fucked your mother."

"What?"

"Your massage-lady mother? Have you?" He looked at me strangely for a moment, but then his face broke open into a wide grin, and he laughed. "I got you, little brother! You should see your face," he sang.

"That's messed up. You're messed up."

Something came over him then. His laughter disappeared and his expression drew inward. "I don't have anything inside me. I don't have anything." He looked shriveled, as if whatever it was that animated him died at that moment. For an instant, I could see what he would look like as an old man.

I reached into my pocket and pulled out the cross I had stolen from my mother's jewelry basket. I held it out to him. "Maybe you can sell it." I dropped the necklace in his hand. I thought about my mother looking in her basket and not finding her necklace. She would be sad. I told myself I didn't care.

FOURTEEN

When Malcolm and I arrived home from Mrs. Poole's house that afternoon, Richard was already there, sitting outside the trailer on one of the beach chairs, drinking from a thirty-two-ounce bottle of Mountain Dew.

"Did you get off early?" I said.

"The job and I had a parting of the ways."

"You got fired?"

"I'm not interested in repairing wind turbines for the rest of my life."

"You only did it for a few weeks."

"Long enough to have experienced it fully. The rest is just repetition and routine."

"What are you going to do now?"

"Right now I think I'll sit here and enjoy this soda and your company, if that's okay with you."

We were still outside when Laurel came home. Malcolm sat in Richard's lap while Richard read out loud from Laurel's dog-eared copy of *Passages*.

"This is a homey picture," she said, smiling. "Although *Winnie the Pooh* would be more like it."

"There's a lot of interesting information in here," Richard said. "Although most of it's dead wrong."

"Like you would know, being an expert about women."

"Hear that, boys? Your mother called me an expert."

"Ha, ha, ha," she said, climbing the stairs to the door.

Malcolm knocked his head back against Richard's chest.

"Oww. Shit," he said, laughing. He banged on Malcolm's head. "What've you got in there?"

"I'm so fat!" Laurel screamed from inside the trailer.

"Hey, that's our baby you're talking about," he called back.

She came to the door wearing cut-off shorts she had left unzipped to accommodate her size. She lifted her man's undershirt to reveal the swollen orb of her stomach. "I'm a whale," she said. "I'm a buoy. I could save your life."

"You already have."

She looked down at herself, smiling proudly. "How come you're home so early?"

DURING DINNER, WE ATE IN tense silence.

"Jobs are jobs. There are a million of them," he said, finally.

"Not here. There aren't a million jobs here. Where we *live*," she said.

"I'll be fine. I always am."

"You say that," she said doubtfully.

"I say it because it's true."

"Depends on your definition of 'fine.' "

"What's that supposed to mean?"

She shook her head, staring down at her plate. "It's not just about you anymore."

"Do you think you need to tell me that? What do you guess I'm doing here anyway? Enjoying the heat?" The threat of an explosion competed with the effortful quiet of his voice. After a long silence, he reached out and brushed Malcolm's hair out of his eyes, then tickled him behind the ears. Malcolm wiggled in his chair.

"Let him eat," she said. "You're distracting him."

"I'm playing with him."

"We're eating. This is dinnertime."

"There sure are a lot of rules in this house."

"Is that a problem for you?"

"It might be."

"Don't do that."

"Do what?"

"Threaten me. This is not conditional," she said. "*This,*" she repeated, clasping her stomach like a basketball, "is not conditional."

"Everything is, honey. Everything."

She sighed and turned toward me. "What happened today?"

"Nothing," I said.

"Ten hours of nothing?"

"Yeah."

"I'm just trying to have a little conversation here, Ares. It's what people do."

"Talk to your mother," Richard said.

"Fuck you."

"Whoa," Laurel said. "Where did that come from?"

"Hey, watch that mouth!" he said.

"I don't want Malcolm to hear that language," she said.

"Why?" I said. "It's not like he's going to imitate it. He doesn't *talk*."

Malcolm moved his arm, and his glass of milk fell over. Instinctively, everyone pushed away from the table. Richard stood, his hands flying into the air as if to prove his innocence. The milk ran quickly off the table onto Malcolm's lap. He began to rock back and forth.

"It's okay," Laurel said, simultaneously throwing her napkin on the spill and reaching for him. She led him to the couch and began to strip off his shirt. His arms flailed at his sides. "Ares, get me some clean clothes for him," she yelled over his shrieks.

I didn't move.

"Did you hear your mother?" Richard said.

"Is this what it's going to be like from now on?" I said. "The two of you against me?"

"What the hell are you talking about? Go help your mother."

"Why don't *you*?"

"Could someone help me here?" Laurel said. She had her arms around Malcolm's naked body, trying to keep him still. "Oww, shit!" She doubled over, her hands on her stomach.

"Laurel?" Richard said, moving quickly to her.

"He kneed me."

"In your stomach?" He took Malcolm by the shoulders. "You *cannot* do that," he said, emphasizing each syllable.

"Don't hurt him," I said.

"You shut up!" Richard said.

"It's okay," Laurel said, sitting up and taking Malcolm from Richard's grasp. "I'm fine. He's upset because of the milk." Malcolm began to moan.

"He kicked you in the stomach."

"It was an accident."

"You should lie down."

"I'm fine. Come on, baby," she whispered to Malcolm. "Take a deep breath."

"I want you to lie down," he repeated. "You need to take care of my baby."

"*Your* baby?" she said, turning to face him. "I was taking care of *your* baby just fine on my own before you showed up. Now suddenly I'm incompetent?"

"That's not what I meant."

"I just need someone to get him some fresh clothes. That is what I need."

I got Malcolm's clean clothes out of his dresser and handed them to her.

"Thank you," she said.

"Looks like you've got it all worked out here," Richard said. "Looks like you don't need me."

"This is exactly what I don't want," she said. "I don't want to take care of you, too."

"Why is it so goddamn hard with you, Laurel? Can you tell me that?"

I left the trailer then. I heard Richard call after me a few times and I heard the beginning of a threat. I got on my bike and rode.

THAT NIGHT, WHEN KEVIN CLIMBED out of his window, I told him I wanted to go with him.

"No."

"You can ride me on the handlebars." I caught his arm. "I'll show you something cool."

Kevin shook me away. "Get off me, man."

"Then forget about taking my bike."

"Screw you."

I ran to the curb and picked up my bike. As I wheeled slowly away, my heart pounded.

"You're a pain in the ass, little brother," he said. He was beside me, breathless from trying to catch up. I slid off the seat, and he got on. Then I hiked myself up on the handlebars.

We fell twice, getting tangled up in each other. He called me a faggot, I called him a sissy and an asshole. I was determined and goaded him back onto the bike after each fall. Finally, when we managed to figure out how to ride without falling, I lifted my arms to either side of me.

"I'm Super-fucking-man!" I called out.

"You're a freak!"

"Would you rather see the future or read minds?"

"See the future," he yelled, breathless from pumping hard. "I don't want to know what shit other people are thinking about me."

"Climb the sides of buildings or breathe underwater?"

"Breathe underwater!"

"Be invisible or fly?"

"Invisible!"

"Invisible! Yes! I want to be invisible too!" We both screamed into the night.

When we finally reached the drainage canal, the bike bucked over some loose rocks and we both flew off.

"This is what you want to show me?" Kevin said after he finished calling me names. "There's nothing here."

I walked around, searching for the landmarks, then sank down and began to dig with my hands until the top layer of soil broke apart, revealing softer dirt beneath it.

"What is this? Buried treasure?" He crouched down and started to dig with me. After a while, I saw a glint of metal.

"Holy shit!" he marveled, working faster until he uncovered the gun. "How did you know it was here?"

"I put it here," I said, and told him the story of the gun and the dead man in the sea.

"It's evidence, little brother," he said, lifting the gun. "You could be thrown in jail for this. You're an accessory."

"Maybe the gun doesn't have anything to do with the dead guy."

"A gun and a dead guy in the water? Put two and two together."

"You can't tell anyone."

"With my record? They'd throw my ass in jail just for *seeing* this." He raised the gun in the air. "Pow," he said softly. "Does it have bullets?"

206 | MARISA SILVER

"I don't know."

He checked the chamber. "Fucking thing is loaded!" He stood and aimed the gun into the distance, then whipped his body around and pointed at another imaginary target. "My name is Bond. James Bond," he said with a bad accent. "You be M," he continued in his normal voice.

"What?"

"Be M. Send me on my mission."

"Okay." I was excited to slip back into the habit of my fantasy games. "There are hijackers about to take over an airplane. You must go and deactivate the bomb before it explodes and kills hundreds of innocent people."

"Got it," he said. "Over and out." He crept around, hiding behind a section of rusted piping, springing up, then dropping back down as if to avoid being seen.

"The hijackers!" I said, pointing. "They're boarding the plane."

"You be them!" he said, running toward the imaginary airplane.

I ran in front of him and did my best to look beady-eyed and shifty.

"Alright! Everybody down!" Kevin said, waving the gun back and forth along an imaginary line of passengers. "If you do what I say, no one will get hurt. No sudden moves!"

I lay down on my stomach, reached for a stick, and held it up.

"What the fuck are you doing?"

"It's the bomb. It's dynamite. I'm the hijacker."

"*I'm* the hijacker."

"You're Bond."

"Get down or I'll blow your fucking head off."

"You can't change the rules."

Kevin pointed the gun at me. "Shut up or I'll have to blow up this airplane and everyone in it."

I stared at the gun; my heart was pounding. Kevin looked at me, but I could tell he wasn't seeing me. He'd gotten lost in the game.

"I'll do it, too," he said. "I don't care what happens to me. Nobody cares what happens to me."

I thought about running, but he might think I was an escaping passenger and shoot me. He continued to aim the gun at my face. His jaw muscles worked and his eyes darted back and forth.

"I quit," I said finally.

Something shifted in his face and he returned, but he still pointed the gun at me. "You can't quit. That's not part of the game."

"I don't want to play anymore." I stood up slowly.

He let the gun fall to his side. "It's cooler to be Bond than a hijacker anyway," he said. Then he turned around and fired the gun. I heard a click, then nothing. "Doesn't work. I guess it drowned, too," he said.

"It's the wrong kind of gun," I said, remembering what Richard had said about the rain in Vietnam.

"Fucking useless," he said, throwing it to the ground.

I picked it up, walked back to the hole, and dropped it in.

"What is this place, anyway?" Kevin said as I filled in the hole and smoothed the dirt over it.

"A drain."

"It smells like shit."

"It's not that kind of drain."

"It still smells like shit," he said, sniffing the air.

I breathed in deeply. The air was touched with something rank and rotten.

FIFTEEN

By the next morning, hundreds of dead fish were washed up on the shore. I stood with Laurel, Richard, and Malcolm on the beach, staring down at grey hulls of tilapia piled on top of one another. The water, teeming with algae, had turned the color of canned peas. Other people wandered through the devastation as though searching for loved ones after a war. The smell of death and rot began to permeate the air, first sweet, then rancid and choking. I pulled the bottom of my T-shirt over my nose and mouth.

"Come on, boys," Laurel said. "Come away from here."

During the next few days, workers from the Parks Department collected the fish in trash bags and took them away, but the odor lingered. At night, I could smell death on my sheets.

The next day, I found her sitting on the trailer steps, rocking gently. Malcolm played by the road, dragging a stick in the dirt. "I'm sad," she said.

"Why?"

"I don't know. The fish, I guess."

"The water's polluted."

Her hands were swollen. She couldn't wear her jewelry anymore, and her fingers bore the ghost shadows of her rings. "It makes me depressed." She reached over and wrapped her hand around my wrist. "I'm scared for this baby."

"Were you scared for me?"

She shook her head. "I was so young. And you were my reassurance."

"That what?"

"That I would never go home again. You anchored me here. Mal, too. But it's such a world. And so much can happen." She looked at me as if waiting for me to say something helpful or give her a solution to her quandary. Did she want me to say I wouldn't make the same mistake twice and drop this new baby, too? Malcolm started down the road.

"Come back here, baby," she called. "Mal?" But he didn't respond. "Goddamn it. Mal!" she muttered.

"I'll get him," I said.

When we returned, he sank into her lap and began to play with a strand of her hair.

She gently pushed his arm away. "No . . . no, baby. I don't want to play."

He sucked in a laugh and continued to twist her hair.

"No! I just . . . I . . . Ares, get him off me. I just . . . I can't have him all over me right now! It's just too much touching. It's too much!" She pushed him off her lap and he tumbled onto the ground. His face contorted, and he opened his mouth, but no sound came out. It was just like that day at the gas station. The silence was horrible.

"Oh my God," she said, covering her face as I went to him. "Oh my God."

A WEEK LATER, THE BIRDS began to die. Malcolm and I stood by the shore where three pelicans lay like torn sheets. Two were dead, but one was still living, although it couldn't move its wings or lift its head. Its chest rose and fell in shallow breaths. Malcolm squatted and gently ran his hand over its body.

"He's resting," I said, hearing the hollowness of my lie. "He's tired out from all the flying. He'll be better soon." He started to lift the bird. "No, Mal," I said, laying a hand on his arm. "You can't take him home." He made a low, heaving sound, and I realized he was crying.

I steered my bike with one hand. The other supported the sling I'd fashioned out of a pillowcase, tying the ends around my neck. The bird rested inside this cradle. Malcolm, on his bike, followed me as I turned toward the park ranger station. I left him and the bird outside the visitor's center and asked the woman at the information desk if I could speak to Mr. Poole.

"Who?"

"Jerry Poole. He works here."

"Is he a volunteer?"

"He's a biologist. He has a badge."

The woman escorted us to another building then told us to wait while she went inside. After a few minutes, Mr. Poole came out of the door. He wore a white clinical coat over his clothes. He looked surprised and then happy to see us, but his expression fell when he saw the bird on Malcolm's lap.

"Where did you get him?"

"Near our house. He's dying."

"Yes," he said. "You shouldn't have moved him. We're taking care of them, as many as we can."

"My brother is upset."

For the first time, Mr. Poole focused on Malcolm. "This is the boy who comes to the house?" He squatted down. Malcolm looked to the side, unable to meet Mr. Poole's gaze. "You're the one who likes birds, huh?" Mr. Poole said.

"He doesn't talk."

"Here," Mr. Poole said, reaching for the bird. Malcolm drew back.

"It's okay, Mal," I said. "Give him the bird. He can make it better."

"I can try," Mr. Poole said.

"Give him the bird, Mal," I repeated. But when Malcolm would not release the bird, my embarrassment got the better of me. "Mal, do it," I said harshly.

"It's okay," Mr. Poole said. "He can carry the bird himself." He reached for Malcolm's shoulder.

"Don't touch him," I said quickly.

Mr. Poole did not react with distress or confusion. He seemed to understand and accept something about Malcolm that most people could never get used to. I put my hand on Malcolm's back. "Come on, man," I said. "He's gonna fix the bird."

A room inside the building had been set up as a makeshift animal hospital. Sick and dying birds lay on all the available surfaces. A few men and women stood over the birds, tending them. The only sound came from people talking in low whispers and the clinking of equipment. The birds made no sound at all.

"Let's put your guy down here," Mr. Poole said to Malcolm, indicating a wooden table covered with a disposable sterile cloth. Surprisingly, Malcolm did what Mr. Poole told him. "You see his eyes?" Mr. Poole continued, talking in a low, confident tone while he prepared a dropper full of medicine. "He can't move them right now. So we have to give him some medicine so his eyes don't get infected." He held the dropper out to Malcolm. When Malcolm took it, Mr. Poole opened the bird's eye.

"Squeeze," I said, helping Malcolm depress the dropper. Some of the liquid squirted over Mr. Poole's hand. "Sorry," I said.

"It's okay. I put in more than he needs." He refilled the dropper, handed it to Malcolm, and carefully turned the bird's head so the other eye was accessible. Without being told, Malcolm squeezed out the medicine again.

"Good job," Mr. Poole murmured. "Now we're going to flush his body," he said. "Get out all the bad stuff." He filled a syringe with water, opened the bird's beak, and squirted the water inside, massaging the neck at the same time. Malcolm reached over and put his hand on the pelican's throat. "That's right," Mr. Poole said. "Help him swallow."

"Is he going to live?" I said.

"I don't know," Mr. Poole said, concentrating on filling

another syringe. "We'll keep him here for a while. With any luck, he'll be out there fishing again."

"Will he be the same as he was? Will he be damaged?"

"We'll tag him and track him. It'll take a while to see how well the rehabilitated ones do back in the world, how strong their systems are after we get the poison out of them."

"What happened to them?"

"All those fish that died the last few weeks? The birds ate the rotten fish and got sick."

"Won't he get sick again? If he eats more fish?"

"Maybe," Mr. Poole said. "Hope not. But we can do our best. We can show him we're not giving up on him."

"Do you think he knows that we didn't give up?"

"I do," Mr. Poole said. "I think every living thing knows when it's cared for."

Malcolm did not put up a fight when it was time to go. He lay his cheek on the bird's body for a few seconds then followed me outside. He was calmer than I'd ever seen him before. But all I could think about was that no matter what you did for one bird, you were going to lose in the end. Bad things would keep happening. Fish would die and birds would eat them. There was no way to stop it. By the time we got home I was suffused with a leaden sadness. I knew what Kevin meant when he said he felt like there was nothing inside him. The feeling exhausted me, rendered me unable to do anything but lie on the couch and watch Malcolm stack books into a pile. It made me into my own audience as I went to the refrigerator for a glass of milk, as I pulled a shirt over my head and prepared for bed. I did all these things thinking:

I am drinking a glass of milk. I am dressing. I am brushing my teeth. I am checking the stove. I thought about the fact that I was doing all those meaningless things at the same time that the world was the way it was.

That night, I stood outside for a long time and looked toward the Chocolate Mountains. Even from that distance, I could see the explosions of people preparing for wars that, at the moment, were only in their imaginations, but that would one day become real.

SIXTEEN

Richard woke early, made eggs and toast, and helped dress Malcolm for school. Laurel moved through the motions of her morning—dressing in her spa uniform, putting her lunch of leftovers in a plastic container—saying nothing. When she was finally ready to leave, she kissed Malcolm.

"I'll be late," she said to me.

"I'll be here," Richard said.

"Of course you will."

"Are we gonna do this now? Again?"

"Maybe."

He looked at her and decided not to push further. "Alright. Let's go, guys. I'll give you a lift." He put a hand on Malcolm's back and guided him to the door.

"I don't want to go with you," I said.

"Don't make things complicated," Laurel said.

"I'll ride my bike."

"Ares, just do what Richard says."

"Hey, that's fine," he said. "He wants to be on his own. I get that."

"This is what I hate," Laurel said, her voice shaking. "I hate other people making decisions for me. I hate it."

"This is between me and Ares. You don't have to worry about it at all."

"Don't do that," she said. "Don't condescend to me. This is my life. I'll worry about what I want to worry about."

"God! I just want to ride my fucking bike to school, Mom."

"Great," she said. "Just great."

That day, I stole a basketball from the gym. When I went onto the yard, I dribbled it all the way to the bike stand. No one asked me where I'd gotten the ball, not even Coach Watson, who passed me as he headed toward his car. All my life I had worried so much about what other people thought of me, but it turned out that nobody really cared what anybody else did. My thefts were futile. I was never in danger of being found out by a world that wasn't looking.

That night, when I rounded the corner of Mrs. Poole's house, I saw lights flickering inside Kevin's darkened room. I tossed a handful of pebbles at his window, but he did not appear. Just as I was about to leave, he pulled aside the drapes and lifted the window. The lights still played in back of him.

"What are you doing?" I said.

"Watching movies."

I leaned into the window. A small projector was set up on the desk, and a grainy, washed-out image played on the wall opposite his bed. On the film, a little boy rode up to the camera on a tricycle and leered into the lens.

"Is that you?"

"Yeah."

He moved back into his room and I hoisted myself through the window. He sat on the edge of his bed, staring at the silent image.

"Whose house was that?" I said, as the image switched to a birthday celebration where four-year-old Kevin, his hair much blonder, wore a paper crown and blew out the candles on a cake. He was surrounded by other children. A woman wearing a printed apron over her dress entered the frame and leaned over him. She looked up at the camera, smiled, and waved. She tried to coax Kevin to do the same, but he was too busy sticking his fingers into the icing.

"Is that your real mother?"

"No."

"Who is it?"

"I don't remember her name. That kid with the big afro was Antoine," he said, pointing to the screen. "I remember him."

The image changed. Kevin, wearing another outfit, rode a scooter down a narrow alley following a girl who rode a tricycle. He pushed hard until he crashed into her and she fell. He turned to the camera as if someone had called to him. He did not look chagrined. He looked like nothing had happened at all. The image tilted down to the ground, swung wildly around, and then went to black. When the picture returned, young Kevin was in a kitchen. He was screaming at someone. He picked up a folding chair and hurled it toward the camera. An adult man came into the frame and grabbed him.

Kevin threw his fists in the air, trying to land a blow. The man turned to the camera and said something, and the image went black.

"What were you mad about?" I asked.

"I don't remember," he said flatly.

The next image showed a group of kids dressed for Halloween.

"I'm the fireman," he said. The camera moved busily as a different woman handed out paper bags to each of the excited children.

Someone knocked on Kevin's door. "Get out of here," he hissed.

"Kevin?" It was Mrs. Poole, speaking from the hallway.

I didn't have time to climb out of the window before the doorknob turned. I slid under the bed.

Mrs. Poole stood in the open doorway. "I saw the lights," she said. I could see her bare feet.

"I was just watching some stuff." The projector was still running and light played across the carpet.

"You look like you were having fun there," she said, moving into the room.

"She wouldn't let us keep our candy. I think she ate it. Look at that fat ass."

"Now, come on," she said, but she was laughing. "You never wanted to trick or treat here."

"It's for kids."

"You're still a kid, you know. You're just fifteen."

"I feel like I'm dead."

"Don't say that."

"Why not?"

"You don't mean it."

"How do you know what I mean? You don't know me."

The film ran out of the projector, and the loose end slapped against the reel until Kevin got up and turned off the machine. The room fell into darkness. He sat down again. There was a long silence.

"Why'd you let me come back here?" he said.

"This is your home."

"I don't have a home."

"I'm sad to hear you say that."

"You know what my home is? Me. I'm my home."

"That's a lonely feeling, I bet."

"How do you know what I feel?"

"You need to be around people who care about you."

"I don't need you!" he said, with sudden vehemence. "I don't need anybody. I don't need any of this shit. This baseball shit and these fucking posters."

"I don't want you to feel that way . . . oh!" she exclaimed. "Oh, you're crying. Don't cry."

"I'm so tired of everything," he said, his voice choked. "I'm so tired."

"I know," she said. "Come here. You're just a baby. Let me . . . I can . . . I can hold you. Will you let me do that?"

"I'm not a baby," he said through his tears.

"Okay. I'm sorry, I'm sorry I said that. I'm just trying to help you."

"Everybody's always trying to help me. But they don't. They just make it worse."

"Make what worse?"

"I hurt!" he wailed. The sound was huge and awful like the sound of an animal in the throes of death.

"Why won't you let me take care of you?"

"I want . . . ," he said, but his words were trapped by his tears.

She sat down on the bed. "Tell me what you want." There was some movement above me. "There," she said. "That's right. You just need to let someone hug you."

The room fell into a silence punctuated only by the sound of his muffled cries and her shushing him. Suddenly, she moved abruptly.

"Stop that! No. You can't do that!" She stood up and moved away from the bed. "You can't . . . what are you doing?"

"You're not my mother," he growled.

"You can't touch me that way. That's disgusting!"

"See? I'm disgusting. I'm sick. You don't give a shit about me."

"That's not what I meant. You're twisting my words."

"Are you gonna tell Jerry now?" he said, mockingly.

"You made a mistake." Her voice shook. "It was a mistake. I know you didn't mean it."

"Are you gonna send me back to the center?"

"I am not giving up on you. Do you hear me? You can be a good boy. I can make you good. I can fix you and make you better."

He moaned as if her words had physically injured him. "Go away. Leave me alone!"

"Fine. If that's what you want." I watched her legs moving to the door.

"Why did you bring me back here?" he cried out, miserably, but she was already gone.

I waited for him to say something to me, but he didn't. I was scared to face him so I stayed under the bed and listened to him sob. His cries were desolate sounds, like the noises Malcolm made. When he quieted, I crawled out from underneath the bed. He sprang up, his surprise evident. His face contorted with rage.

"What the fuck are you doing here?" He lunged at me and pushed me up against the wall. Then he brought his hands to either side of his head as if he were trying to block out a loud sound. "I gotta get out of here," he said. He threw open the window. I climbed out after him and ran to the bike, but he was faster.

"I want to go home," I said as he mounted the bike. He pushed off and began to pedal. "Please," I begged, running beside him. I reached for the handlebars and managed to throw him off balance. He stopped before he fell. "At least ride me home," I said. He didn't put up a fight, so I lifted myself onto the handlebars.

He pedaled hard and the bike flew down the road. We traveled along the highway toward Bombay Beach. Before we reached the turnoff, he stopped at a small cluster of houses set back from the road. I jumped down from the handlebars. He wheeled the bike to a dilapidated house that looked no bigger than a shack. I reached for the bike, but he grabbed my arm and pulled me toward the front door. The door opened and I looked up into the face of Calvin Epps.

"What did you bring him for?" he said.

"Where's Ronnie?" Kevin said, pushing past Calvin and bringing me into the house. The living room was dominated by an enormous red sofa and a coffee table shaped like the number eight. A poster of Muhammad Ali looking poised to throw a punch hung behind the couch, its corners curling away from the wall. The house smelled like leftover fast food. Duane came into the living room, took one look at me, and glanced at Calvin, who shrugged.

"Where's your brother?" Kevin said. He tapped his foot quickly against the floor.

"Doing some business."

"Is he here?"

"Looks like someone's freaking out," Calvin said.

"Is he here or not?" Kevin said.

"Is who here?"

I looked over to see Ronald standing in the doorway. His leather jacket hung on his shoulders in a way that made me think it had once belonged to a bigger man. His mustache accentuated his drawn face and sunken cheeks. He walked into the house and handed a paper bag to Calvin, who removed a jar of cheese spread and a box of Triscuits from it and tossed the bag on the floor.

"Hey! This is my house, man. Use a fucking garbage can," Ronald said, and Calvin quickly picked up the bag.

Calvin sat down on the couch next to Duane, and the two started eating.

Ronald looked me over. "I've seen you," he said.

"He lives around here," Kevin said.

"Him and that retard kid," Calvin said.

"No." Ronald squinted as if trying to see me more clearly. "I've seen you two together. In that truck. With that guy."

"Kid was snooping around my house," Kevin said. "We had to take him home."

"Who's the driver?"

"This guy I have to live with."

"He a cop?" Ronald said.

"Fuck no," Kevin said.

"Is he?" Ronald said, directing the question to me.

"He's a biologist."

Calvin and Duane hooted, crackers spluttering out of their mouths.

Ronald studied me for a while longer, then crossed the room.

"I need something," Kevin said. "I really need something, like, right now. I'm, like, all fucked up."

Ronald disappeared into the kitchen. I heard the refrigerator open then close. He reappeared carrying a bottle of beer. He sat down on a folding chair and took his time drinking. Kevin was jumpy and picked his face. Duane lit up a joint and passed it to Calvin.

"Share the wealth, little brother," Ronald said.

Reluctantly, Calvin reached over and handed the joint to Kevin.

"That's not what I want."

"Looks like it's what you need," Ronald said. "Something to smooth you out. You're a nervous motherfucker."

"You got any black beauties?"

"Pass it on," Ronald said of the joint.

Kevin took a quick hit and passed me the joint. Calvin and Duane watched me. "Look at the kid," Duane said. "He's about to shit his pants."

I remembered looking up into his face as he landed a kick in my stomach. I had been inconsequential to him, such an easy target. I might have been an empty soda can or a piece of wood. I could tell he and Calvin would relish a chance at me again. I put the joint to my lips and inhaled. The smoke burned my throat, but I managed not to gag. I didn't feel anything except the heat, which fanned out through my chest. The joint was passed around a few more times, and Kevin began to calm. He sat down next to Calvin.

"You look uncomfortable," Ronald said to me. "Are you uncomfortable?"

"No." I felt a small buzzing in my head, as if the lining of my brain were vibrating very softly.

"You're making me uncomfortable," Ronald said. He took a gun out of his jacket pocket and set it on the table. Then he pulled out a baggie and poured out some pills. Kevin lunged for them, but Ronald caught his hand. "I'll take some money."

Kevin reached into his pocket. He counted out some wrinkled bills and gave them to Ronald, who looked like he was expecting more.

"I just want one," Kevin said.

"You're not going to buy something for your friend? That's not very polite."

"He doesn't care."

"Maybe he's going to run home and tell mommy."

"He's not."

"You can take back your cash, brother," Ronald said, scooping up the pills. "I don't need the trouble."

Kevin shot me a look, considered his options, and handed Ronald more money. Ronald picked up two pills, handed one to me, but held on to Kevin's. "Guests go first," he said when Kevin protested.

"Do it," Kevin said to me.

I held the pill between my fingers and hesitated. Calvin laughed.

"Eat it!" Kevin said.

Inertia washed over me. I had seen too much that day, more than I could understand. There seemed to be no way out of my situation, no way out of the life I had fallen into. Suddenly I didn't care what happened to me. I put the pill in my mouth, threw back my head, and swallowed.

The next thing I knew, my body was spring-loaded. My heart beat so fast I thought I could see my shirt twitch. I couldn't stop moving. I laughed but I wasn't happy. I talked but I didn't know what I was saying. Someone put music on, and I threw myself against the walls and onto the couch and other people, but I couldn't hear what was playing. Every cell in my body felt like it was bumping up against every other cell.

I don't know how long we stayed in that house or when

the decision was made to leave, but the next thing I knew, I was in a car, and someone was yelling: "Not in the car! Not in the car!" A hand pushed my head out the opened window. I retched and saw my trail of vomit break apart in the wind. Then someone pushed me out onto the ground, and the car drove away. My bike lay next to me. I looked up and saw the one red and one green Christmas light of our trailer winking on and off.

I made it to the bathroom in time to vomit again. I flushed the toilet and leaned weakly against the wall. My head was still buzzing. I couldn't locate myself, couldn't tell if I was sitting up or lying down. I was having thoughts but they were coming from outside me. My self was lost. I knew, finally, what it was like to be my brother. Malcolm was lost not only among people, but also inside his own body. And there was no way out. I was terrified. *Count.* I told myself. *One, two, three* . . . Malcolm counted pennies, pebbles, buttons from Laurel's lost button box. *Four, five, six* . . . The numbers kept building up, but I felt no calmer. *Twenty-one, twenty-two* . . . The numbers would never end. *Twenty-three, twenty-four* . . . Was this what Malcolm felt every second of his life? Did he feel like he would suffocate inside the empty white prison of his brain? Was he as scared as I was now?

"Hey, now. Hey," Richard whispered in my ear. He lifted me up and carried me to my bed and lay me down. "What happened to you?" He looked into my eyes and saw his answer. He shook his head wearily, pulling the covers up to my chin, and laid his hand on my forehead. "It'll be out of your system in the morning."

"Are you going to tell her?"

"She has enough problems."

He started to take his hand away but I held on to it. "Stay."

He sat down at the edge of my bed. "Okay. I'm right here."

SEVENTEEN

At school, I felt like I was swimming. Kids moved up and down the halls, their boisterous conversations coming at me as if through water. I thought about raising my hand in social studies but decided not to because what did it matter if I knew the right answer? What did it mean? At the end of fourth period, rather than going to math, I left the building, emerging into the crash of sunlight that reflected off the roofs of the cars in the parking lot. A maintenance man stood on a ladder next to the school's announcement sign. One by one, he affixed big plastic letters to the board, using long metal pincers. I watched until I figured out that the letters were going to form the words "Go Team!" I started to laugh.

I went back to school at dismissal to get Malcolm. The only person in room 23 was Mrs. Murphy, sitting at a child-sized desk.

"We were looking for you," she said.

"Where's my brother?"

She looked up at me. She had been crying. "I didn't know," she said. "There are so many kids. I didn't know."

MALCOLM AND I WERE SITTING outside the principal's office when Richard arrived. He looked at us but said nothing. He took off his hat and rubbed his head self-consciously, hunching his shoulders as he approached the secretary's desk as though embarrassed by the formality of the office. "Their mother is at work," he said.

"And you are?"

"I'm their mother's . . . I'm a family friend."

"I'll let Principal Philipson know you are here."

Malcolm and I waited while Richard and Philipson talked inside the office. When they emerged, Richard motioned for us to follow them. Philipson led us outside the school and across the yard to a place I was familiar with—it was the place Malcolm always went when he escaped his class. Now the area was blocked off by wooden construction horses. As we approached, the air thickened with a familiar smell of rot.

"Have a look," Philipson said.

The hole was filled with dead birds. Most of the birds were small, no larger than a hand. They lay together like old men in overcoats, huddling against the cold.

"I don't understand," Richard said.

"Malcolm dug this hole," Philipson said.

"Malcolm likes to dig," Richard said. "He's a world-class digger. Looks like he found something strange here."

"He didn't just find this," Philipson said. "He put them here. Another student saw him kill a bird."

"How would he do that?" Richard said.

"With a shovel."

Richard was quiet. His eyes darted back and forth, as if he were looking for a way to escape without divulging his intention. "Why did he bury them?" he said, uncertainly.

The answer, I knew, was that Malcolm remembered when I buried the gun. He thought that is what you did with your secrets.

Richard was silent. He folded his arms over his chest, then let them drop by his sides as if he sensed they were useless to him now. He turned to me. "Did you know about this?"

"No."

"He started to defend this area," Philipson said. "He wouldn't let the other children near it. He became aggressive."

"He gets confused," Richard said.

Philipson said nothing.

Richard inhaled, drew himself up. "Look, the kid has problems. We know that already." Then he let go of the air, and with it his resolve. "He's a good kid," he said. "A sweet kid."

"He's been killing birds," Philipson said.

"No!" I said. "He loves birds. He wants to *be* a bird."

"We really don't know that," Philipson said.

"*I* know that. I know what he thinks."

Philipson smiled grimly at Richard. "Okay, kiddo," Richard said, placing a silencing hand on my shoulder. "Let's not make this worse than it is."

I stared into the open grave. The birds looked cozy and peaceful, as if they had found a way to ward off life's whimsy by bundling together in death.

That afternoon, I sat on my bed, my stolen objects on my lap, fingering the palm tree key chain, the deck of cards. Richard and Laurel stood outside the trailer by my open window.

"I said we'd look into getting him help," Richard said.

"Help?"

"He killed birds."

"A bird," she says. "They saw him kill one bird."

"Why don't you want to help him?"

"Excuse me?"

"It's like you're content to let him be this way."

"I like him this way. I *love* him this way. Maybe I'm the only one."

"But you're not. That's just what you decided. Everyone else is the enemy. Everyone else wants to hurt him. But you're the one."

"I'm the one what?"

"You're hurting him."

"He's safe here. I can keep him safe."

"I don't think that's what's going on here. I don't think you're keeping *him* safe. I mean, look around, Laurel. This isn't paradise, you know."

"Fuck you," she said softly.

"I'm not the one who's getting fucked."

"Get out," she said, her growl low and commanding.

"Laurel—"

"I want you to go."

The door of the Jeep slammed shut, and Richard drove away. I looked down at the useless objects in my lap. Everything around me was falling apart. My life felt broken, and there was nothing in the house, no person, who could keep me safe.

I left the trailer. Laurel was hugging herself, staring at the empty space where Richard's Jeep had been. When I told her I was taking a ride, she didn't respond. Inside the trailer, something clattered to the floor—a pile of books, maybe, or a chair. Malcolm started to moan. Laurel still did not move.

"Mom? Are you going to help him?"

"I guess not," she said.

I imagined leaving him alone with her. What would happen if he cried and cried and she did not move to calm him? Would he be trapped that way forever? I was scared for him. I was scared for both of us. "I'm going to take him with me," I said.

She didn't answer.

AT THE DRAINAGE DITCH, I threw down my bike, sank to my knees, and began to dig. Malcolm stood nearby, uninterested in what I was doing. The ground was surprisingly soft, as if it had been recently turned. My heart sank. I pulled at the loose dirt. Nothing was there. The gun was gone.

Mrs. Poole opened her door. I hadn't seen her since the

night I'd hidden under Kevin's bed. She seemed taken aback to see us. "This isn't Malcolm's day."

"Where's Kevin?

"He has a bike now." She said this in such a way that I wondered whether he had exacted the bike as a bribe.

"I left something in his room. Something for school."

She sighed and opened the door further and let me and Malcolm pass.

In Kevin's room, I quickly searched through the desk drawers and behind the books on the shelf, but I did not find the gun. I opened the closet and looked in the dark corners where he had thrown balled-up shirts and orphaned socks.

"What the fuck?"

It was Kevin, standing in his doorway, his face flushed from riding his bike.

"Where is it?" I said, standing up.

"Get out of my room."

"Give me the gun."

A strange smile crept across his face. He reached into the waistband of his pants and pulled out the weapon.

Malcolm started moaning softly.

"Shut up," Kevin snapped at him. He waved the gun. "Get out of my room."

Malcolm's moans grew more insistent.

"Get him to shut up!" Kevin said, growing agitated.

"Give me my gun."

Malcolm started to rock in place. Kevin's anger and distress grew, and I recognized the look on his face. He was disappearing into someplace dangerous. Malcolm started to flap his hands, and Kevin crossed the room and pushed Malcolm so hard that Malcolm fell back, hitting his head against the wall. The sound of his head striking something hard and unforgiving pierced me; I had heard it night after night for five years. I threw myself at Kevin and knocked him off balance. He grabbed hold of me and brought me down with him. As we fought, the gun fell from his hands. He rolled on top of me and began to shake me. My head struck the floor over and over. He grabbed my throat and began to tighten his grip. I couldn't breathe. He squeezed harder still. As I began to lose consciousness, I saw the deadness in his eyes. And then a sound exploded in the room. Kevin collapsed on top of me. His grip loosened. Gasping, I turned my head, and saw my brother, holding the gun by his side. It slipped from his fingers and fell to the ground as if it were one of the fake guns from our fantasy games I had fitted into his hand that no longer held his fickle attention.

What I did next, I did without thought. I slipped out from under Kevin. I reached for the gun. I took my shirt and wiped the metal so that Malcolm's fingerprints would disappear. I put the gun in my own hand and closed my fingers around it. And then it was done.

WE STAYED IN THAT ROOM. I heard the wail of a distant ambulance and the short coyote barks of police sirens. Mrs. Poole wept while she held Kevin. His long body lay across her lap and she cradled his head, brushing the hair off his forehead again and again. His shirt and her hands were

EIGHTEEN

When the police questioned me at the station, my voice was still raw from having been choked. I was scared, not because I was worried about what would happen to me, but because I did not want to make a mistake and reveal my lie. Laurel was not allowed to be with me, but once, when a policeman left the room, I saw her sitting in the hallway. She wore her faded blue sarong. Her hands rested on the mound of her stomach. Her face was uncommonly pale, her hair unkempt. She looked alone and forlorn and lost. Afterward I was taken to the hospital, where a doctor examined my neck and head, and someone took photographs of my injuries. Malcolm was already there with Richard. His head had been photographed, too. We were finally released from the hospital. My head was bound in gauze.

Once we were home, Laurel and Richard put Malcolm to bed. Afterward, she came through the card curtain and sat down on the edge of my mattress. I looked up at her, and my tears came so suddenly I didn't have a chance to stop them. She reached for me.

"I'm sorry," she said, rocking me. "I'm so sorry."

I remembered those words from years before, when we were at the hospital and Malcolm was bandaged beyond recognition. She had held me and apologized for something I had done, as if the fault were hers.

AT THE DETENTION HEARING, A judge questioned me about the events of the night, and I answered calmly, remembering all that I had said to the police. I was not frightened anymore. Richard and my mother sat in the small courtroom. Mr. and Mrs. Poole sat behind them.

The judge had already asked how I found the gun and I had told him.

"Why did you shoot Kevin?" he asked me.

"Because he was hurting my brother," I said.

"You would do anything to save your brother from harm?"

"He's my brother," I said.

"Did you understand, at the time, that guns kill people?"

I looked at my mother. I could see her shake her head imperceptibly. I knew she wanted me to lie.

"I know about guns," I said.

"What did you feel when you shot the gun?" the judge asked.

"I felt . . . I felt . . ." I stopped. This is a question I had not been asked, and I had no ready answer for it. I had never shot a gun, had never even raised the gun I buried in order to pretend to shoot it. I had only fired sticks in my fantasy games with Malcolm. I thought about what Malcolm might have felt holding that gun and pulling the trigger. Maybe he felt the same way he did when he buried all those birds behind the school.

"I just wanted to make him safe," I said. "Because there are so many bad things that can hurt him."

"Yes, there are," the judge said.

A fantasy scrolled out in my head as rich as any I had created over the years. "And when I shot the gun," I said, imagining myself in Malcolm's moment, "I felt like I saw the whole truth of things."

"What truth?"

"That nothing can really make you safe."

The judge said nothing. The courtroom was quiet. I looked at Laurel. Her hands covered her mouth. Her eyes were glistening oceans.

I was put under house arrest, then brought back to court for a dispositional hearing, where I learned that Mr. and Mrs. Poole had decided not to press charges against me. The district attorney, after conferring with the judge and in view of the Pooles' decision, dropped the State's case. Still, I was not yet free. Because of my action and my family circumstances, the judge ordered me to a therapeutic facility.

I never knew why the Pooles did not care to see the case brought to trial. Perhaps after seeing the evidence of Kevin's violence toward me and my brother, they reconsidered. Or maybe, after so much struggle, they finally gave up on the dangerous boy they had tried and failed to make their son.

NINETEEN

The seven boys from cottage 8 at the Oak Glen Juvenile Improvement Center sat in a loose circle on metal folding chairs inside the group therapy meeting room. The chairs were purple and pink, the same colors I had noticed on the outside of the building when I first came to visit Kevin and mistook the place for a department store. I stared between my legs at the cream-colored linoleum squares flecked with red, green, and blue. I started to count the specks but stopped because doing this reminded me of Malcolm, and of how much I missed my home. I had passed the halfway mark of my court-appointed time here. I had one month left.

It was Lenny's turn to share. He told the story of how his mother dropped him off at his grandparents' house one day, telling him she was going grocery shopping, and how she never came back. He talked about his grandparents, how they took care of him and bought him clothes and some toys, but he hated them anyway. He hated the way his grandfather chewed his food. Lenny did an imitation of the snicking, mucous sounds of that chewing, which made us boys laugh and take the opportunity to make sounds of our own until Dr. Hall and Dr. Gonzalez told us to quiet down. They reminded us about R.E.A.L.: respect, empathy, attentiveness, and love, the four rules we had to abide by in group therapy if we wanted to succeed and graduate from the center. Lenny continued. He told us that he thought about killing his grandparents in their beds by suffocating them with their own pillows.

As he talked, he focused on the peach-colored wall just beyond where Dr. Hall sat, her grey hair tied up in her customary bun. Dr. Gonzalez, his complexion as bumpy as melted plastic, sat next to her, writing notes on a pad or nodding his head to encourage Lenny to keep going. Both leaders occasionally said they "wondered" this or that about Lenny's feelings, as they did when any boy told his crime history, as if our stories were fairy tales meant to elicit awe. It was only because Lenny got caught for the lesser offense of stealing his grandfather's 600 Series Grasshopper lawn mower and trying to sell it to drug dealers, and because it turned out that his grandparents actually did like him, that they didn't press charges and that he was placed at the center rather than in juvenile detention.

"I wonder how your grandparents would feel if they woke up and saw you were trying to murder them?" Dr. Hall asked. She had a way of saying the most awful things as though she were asking for a medium Coke at McDonald's.

* * *

THE NEXT WEEK IT WAS my turn to share. I told my story as I had told it to the police and the judge. I concentrated so hard on telling it correctly that I began to believe it myself.

"I wonder what you felt when you saw that you had killed Kevin?" Dr. Gonzalez said, his heavy-framed glasses reflecting the overhead fluorescents so that I couldn't see his eyes.

It was that same question the judge had put to me. The more I was asked it, and the more I thought about it, the more I began to experience myself in that moment as if it actually *had* been me who killed Kevin. I could feel my hand on the gun, the pressure of the trigger against my finger as I pulled it. I could feel the kickback as the gun fired, could hear the deafening sound of the shot. Each night, when I lay on my bed in cottage 8 listening to the other boys whisper and laugh and occasionally groan, I asked myself the same question I had been asking ever since the day Kevin died. Did Malcolm know what he was doing? Was he guilty? Could he pull a trigger on a gun, feel that power resonate through his body, and be innocent? All the years I had played at war and killing . . . was it really Malcolm all along who was the better soldier? Was he the one who believed the story of good and evil while I was lost in the confusion of right and wrong?

"Ares, I asked you how you felt when you killed Kevin," Dr. Gonzalez said.

"I didn't know what I had done," I said.

"For how long?" Dr. Hall said.

"For a while. I knew that everything was crazy in the room, everybody yelling and screaming. And then suddenly everything was quiet and nobody moved."

"How did that make you feel?"

"Relieved."

"Relieved because Kevin was dead?"

"Relieved because my brother was safe."

"What about Kevin?" Dr. Hall said.

I looked around. All the other boys in the group were staring at me, wondering what I was going to say. For weeks, I had listened to their stories. One boy had been molested by his uncles and had molested his own brother. Another had been beaten up so many times by his father that he was permanently deaf in one ear.

"I hurt him," I said.

"Kevin?" Dr. Gonzalez said. "You killed him, Ares."

"My brother. I dropped him."

And I told the story. The words flew from my mouth as if they were worried I would take them back if they came out any slower. I described the gas station, the heat, the smell of Malcolm's diaper. I made a cradle with my arms as though I were holding my baby brother. When I reached the moment when he kicked me, I could feel him slipping through my grasp. I could hear the *thunk* of his body as it hit the ground.

I stopped, surprised to find myself standing. Everyone in the room was watching me. A look passed between the doctors.

"You feel responsible for the way Malcolm is," Dr. Gonzalez said.

"I am responsible. It's my fault."

The two adults exchanged a look. "I wonder," Dr. Hall said, softly, "if we can talk about that more."

THAT WEEKEND, ON PARENTS' VISITING day, Dr. Hall told me that she was going to have a conference with Laurel first, and that I should wait outside her office. Malcolm, who had come to see me each week, sat in a chair next to me in the hallway, playing with marbles that Laurel had brought to keep him occupied. Now that the truth of what I had done to my brother was out in the open, I was scared that Dr. Hall had decided that I needed to spend more time at the center.

When the door opened, only Dr. Hall appeared. "Ares, why don't you go inside and spend some time with your mother."

I rose uncertainly and did what she said. Once I was in the room she shut the door. My mother sat in front of Dr. Hall's desk with her back to me. She held her head in her hands.

"Mom?"

She turned. She grabbed my hand and pulled me so that I was standing before her. She looked up at me. "Is it true?" she said. "Is it true you told the doctors that you hurt your brother?"

I was too scared to say to her what I had said in the therapy room only a few days earlier. I couldn't believe that finally, after all these years, she was going to confront me.

"Is that what you think, baby?" she said. She tried to fix a smile on her face, but I could tell that she was fighting back tears. "Do you think you hurt him?"

"I dropped him," I whispered. "I'm sorry."

"Kids fall all the time. Didn't you know that?"

"That's why he is the way he is."

"No . . . no. Why would you think that was the reason?"

"You never gave me another reason. You never took him to a doctor. You said he wasn't retarded. You said we couldn't use that word."

"Oh, no. Oh, no," she said. I couldn't tell if she was talking to me or herself. She seemed to withdraw into her thoughts, and her eyes flickered back and forth as if she were watching a film of our whole life up to that point, looking for the moment when mistakes had been made.

"Mom?"

She looked at me. "It's not your fault," she said. "You have to believe me. Do you believe me?"

"What's wrong with him?"

"It's just the way he came into the world. I thought you knew that. Oh, God. I thought you knew."

I LEARNED HOW TO SWING on the high rings in the yard. After a few weeks of trying, the blisters on my hands hardened into calluses, and I could glide from one end of the apparatus to the other for what felt like forever. The feeling was exhilarating. I felt free. When I was in the air I thought about playing games with Malcolm, about Sundays in the desert with my mother, about her hand on my head. I never beat Kevin's record of one hundred passes. It seemed an impossible feat, and there were times when I thought Mrs. Poole must have exaggerated his accomplishment. I wondered if she had done it because she wanted him to be a different kind of son, and because she wanted to be a different kind of mother, one who could be proud of her child's small victories just like real mothers were. Sometimes, when I built up momentum on the rings, I imagined I could let go and fly over the wall of the center all the way back to Bombay Beach and my home.

TWENTY

After my release, a reporter from the newspaper in San Diego came to our house. Laurel would not speak to him. She locked the trailer door and threatened to call the police. I sat by the window and watched the young man in beige chino slacks and a white button-down shirt wander beyond our house into the desert. I saw him stop and turn a full circle, taking the measure of the place we lived. He had a pad, which he wrote on, and a camera, which he used to take photos of our trailer. He turned to the desert to take more pictures, but he must not have seen anything he thought would be meaningful to his readers because he never raised the camera to his eye.

The Pooles had moved away by that time, and the young reporter had only been able to interview people with no knowledge about what had happened except for the gossip that had become fanciful as it made its way from one mouth to another. I was amazed by all the students who spoke to the reporter about me with such assurance when these same kids barely knew me. According to the article that was later published, I was a quiet, heroic boy who had saved the life of my innocent, damaged brother who could do nothing for himself. We lived in a poverty I did not recognize, but that the reporter wrote was "singular," even though our lives were no different from our neighbors. We had what we needed, and my mother knew how to make treasures out of the land that the reporter dismissed as "vacant" and "ruined."

THE JUDGE ORDERED ME TO complete my school year after I returned from the center. Those two weeks were a horror house of taunts and whispers, and a kind of isolation I had never experienced. On the last day of school, I burst out of the doors, eager to leave that place. Richard was waiting in the parking lot for me. Malcolm stood beside the Jeep with him, his bike lying on the ground by his feet. My pleasure at seeing Richard was punctured as I drew nearer. His duffel bags were piled on the backseat.

"You're leaving," I said.

"It's not working out, Ares."

I fought to keep my voice steady. "What about the baby?"

"She did alright with the two of you without a bunch of dumb-ass men around to mess things up," he said, his mouth searching for a smile. But he gave up quickly, and his face and voice dropped. "It's what she wants."

"Fuck you," I said, but my voice broke over the words.

"Hey, hey," he said. "I know you're upset."

"I'm not upset."

"I'm upset, too."

"You were never going to stay to begin with."

He started to contradict me, but stopped. "Maybe not," he said.

"Come on, Mal," I said, reaching down to right his bike then heading toward the racks where my own stood. "We're gonna ride. Fast, fast."

We rode to the sea and when we arrived, I threw my bike to the ground and ran down to the edge of the water. "I AM THE GOD OF WAR!" I yelled. "I AM THE GOD OF WAR!" I let out a roar that came from so deep a place inside me, it was as though my body were a vast cavern that defied physical reality and that held inside it all the space and energy in the universe. And then, like an echo, I heard a roar that mimicked my own so perfectly I thought I had made it. But Malcolm had made this second sound. It was his voice, full of his own feeling. I looked at him and my heart grew inside my chest because I was certain that my brother was not lost as I had feared he was. He had a voice, a pure, true voice that sang the world back to itself. It was the best thing a voice could be called upon to do.

Our sounds frightened a clutch of birds from their hiding place inside a floating tangle of box thorn branches. They exploded just as the children had only an hour earlier, when the final bell of the year rang and they rushed outside, finally free. Malcolm shrieked and threw his hands up as if he wanted to embrace the birds. I watched his delight. It was impossible to believe there was no thought in that boy, that he did not have need or desire or the urge to reach out and touch a wider world in the same way I did. He wanted to

connect to the birds even if it meant killing them and bury-
ing them, keeping them safe from the incessant harms that
came of living. And it was impossible to believe that he did
not have some personal language that expressed what was
central to his being. Perhaps they were not words because
maybe there were none that could say what needed to be
said. There was only the heart expanding with its inability to
contain all the joy and sorrow that it had to hold. It was an
impossible task for any heart. Finally, there was nothing to
do but hold up your arms and scream as loud as you could in
order to let the air and the dirt, the ageless fossils and dried
up fish skeletons know that you were there, trying over and
over to say what could never be said. Malcolm twirled and
fell to the ground laughing his inside-out laugh, and I
laughed with him.

TWENTY-ONE

2007

I hold my brother in a box by the shore of the Salton Sea. What I once took to be sand is simply a stretch of rocks and crushed shells and the detritus of the thousands of fish that have perished in the water over the years. The sea, once filled with the possibility of something whose farther shores could not be seen, is what it always was: an over-salinated and polluted mistake. The land around me is forsaken, a crossroads of the dispossessed. Economic improvements in the country at large must find this place last, when the coffers are empty, or nearly so. This desert outpost is like a child who has found himself such a good hiding spot that he unintentionally exiles himself from the game.

The water, which looks like a blue oasis from a distance is, up close, a murky greenish brown. The gentle but insistent movement of it pushes algae and a disturbing, toxic-looking foam onto the beach. Trash is scattered around the shoreline—a crushed Coke can, a candy wrapper faded by the sun, indestructible Styrofoam food containers that are the clues some future anthropologist will use to determine who we were and what we cared about. But there's not as much trash as you would think because there are still people living here who love this sea as much as we once did, who care about the place they live in even if it is overlooked by almost everyone, even if it exists only as a result of a colossal historic error. There will always be people like my mother who love a mistake, who will claim it, coddle it, and grow it until it has a purpose of its own, until they forget its erroneous beginnings and it becomes something necessary, something they can't live without. This sea has its champions the way stray dogs have rescuers, people who turn up their noses at the breeding of purebreds when there are so many castoff, frightened mongrels lurking beneath underpasses and beside freeways.

The judge in my case took the reporter's view of my heroism, and in view of my youth, and of what was revealed to be a long history of violence on Kevin's part dating from his earliest childhood, he only doled out the barest of punishments, as if it were not a life I had taken but a box of chocolates or a new pair of sneakers from the rack of a cut-rate store. The judge had words for my mother, though. He ordered her to watch Malcolm more closely and to provide him with more expert care. We moved away from Bombay Beach not long after Richard left. We settled into an apartment in San Diego, and my brother Angelo was born there. A new neighbor offered to watch Malcolm while my mother and I took a taxi to the unfamiliar hospital. The doctor gave her a shot and told her not to push until he returned, then left the room. The nurse attached a monitor to Laurel's belly. I held up the long tongue of paper, and Laurel delighted in the peaks and valleys. We pretended our new baby was climbing a mountain on his way to us.

"Don't push," the nurse warned. "The doctor said—"

But Laurel's scream drowned out any further instructions. The nurse pushed up the sheet covering Laurel, then ran to the door, calling, "It's a flyer!" and suddenly I was holding a slippery, warm being in my arms. The baby was taken from me so quickly I hardly realized what had happened. My hands and arms were streaked with blood. I looked at Laurel because I needed her to tell me what to do, just as I had when I was four and had submerged my arms into a bucket of green paint she was using to reinvigorate a yard sale table. Back then she had laughed when I told her I wanted to become an alien. In the hospital room, her face opened in delight, and she laughed, and I laughed, just as we had those many years ago.

"Good catch!" she said.

She named him Angelo because he flew into the world. Richard's last name was Pardee. Angelo Pardee.

Richard came to stay for periods of time, but as the years passed the empty spaces between his visits grew longer until he hardly came at all. Malcolm moved to his first group home when he was twelve, after he had tried to smother Angelo with a plastic bag. The day Malcolm walked inside the doors of that first facility, Laurel looked as though all the bones in her face had been broken at once and her features were falling in on themselves. Everything I recognized about her disappeared in that moment of her defeat. I was eighteen then and had managed to win a scholarship to a state school up north. I was ready to leave my mother, but it frightened me to see her so adrift. Some still childish part of me relied on her obstinate assurance that Malcolm was fine, that we were fine, and that the life we led, and the place where we had lived, despite newspapermen's deprecations and our life's obvious privations, were worth defending as tenaciously as she had defended them for so many years.

It was only when I moved away from my mother and met people who thought about the world in ways wholly different from the way she did, when I studied in earnest and began to read the kinds of books that lined Mrs. Poole's shelves, that I began to try to really understand what those psychiatrists at the center had told me: that my brother's condition had nothing to do with that long-ago accident. There was a time when I was seeing a woman in Davis who was studying child development. I got drunk one night and told her how I had hurt Malcolm, and she brought out books and lecture notes. I read those books, and then others, and I learned all I could about the kind of child my brother was. Sometimes, even now, I run across a television program about children like Malcolm, and I watch obsessively, moving close to the screen as recognition washes over me in waves. I listen to experts explain about disrupted brain chemicals and damaged synapses, about the microscopic dings on a strand of DNA. I watch anguished, brave parents who dedicate themselves to treatments at the expense of financial security, jobs, and sometimes marriages. But what I focus on most are the children who people the backgrounds of the images. I look for the brothers and sisters of the affected child and study how they play and eat and occasionally demand attention, but mostly how they behave as any normal child would, happily ignorant of the evident strangeness around them because it is what they are used to. I wonder if they carry secret burdens in their young hearts. Watching those children, I am awed by the power of their natures to defend them, and I wonder why I was not so protected. Thirty years ago, there was just my brother Malcolm, and what I believed I had done to injure him, and there was my mother's fierce and sometimes neglectful love for us.

I left that decent woman in Davis as I have left many good women who wanted children, or homes, or more of me than I was willing to give them. My college money only took me through two years. The rest of my learning has come from libraries and the people I have traveled among and worked next to, all of whom have stories. I find that if I listen well, their tales, which appear to be about strangers and places I have never been, are about me, too. I have lived throughout the West, in Alaska, Washington, and Idaho, and now seem to have come to roost in Wyoming in the arms of a woman named Margaret who wants children, and a home, and all of me. I finally feel ready. I have chosen to live in a place where the winters are as cold as the desert summers are hot. On certain days of the year, I think that every cell in my brain will be numbed by the knifelike freeze that settles over the mountains. But there is no cold that can erase the heat and desolation of my desert childhood, and of what happened here.

IT TOOK ME EIGHTEEN HOURS to drive from Wyoming to San Diego. I drove straight through, stopping once in St. George, Utah, and then again outside Barstow just to sleep for twenty minutes in my car. I left my home within a half hour of getting the news of Malcolm's death. I don't know why I hurried. Malcolm was gone, after all. There was nothing more I could do for him. But as the miles between us closed, I grew more anxious to arrive. I felt his need for me prickling my skin as I did when I was young and knew that I was responsible for him. When I saw the cityscape of San Diego, a giddy anticipation rocketed through my body as if I were going to greet a lover after a long separation.

I arrived at the group home in the late morning. The director, a big, athletic man who looked as if he would come out on top of any number of situations, showed me to Malcolm's room. I had been in this small, sparse room during my visits, which I tried to make every three or four months, although often the time between them was longer. The only decorations were two generic paintings of mountains and flowers that the staff had hung on the walls. My brother had

become a fastidious man. His bed was neatly made. His two
dress shirts hung side by side in the closet, swaying in the
breeze created when I opened the door. His three pairs of
shoes—a pair of sneakers, shower shoes, and a pair of dress
shoes so seldom worn they reminded me of the shoes children wore to church—were lined up in a straight row on the
closet floor.

My earlier visits to my brother were usually unsatis-
fying. Whether it was the progress of his particular afflic-
tion or the dulling effects of his drug regimens, he turned
more inward with age. He walked with his head bent, as
though he were searching for something he'd lost, and he
tended to drag his feet. His posture and shuffling gait
became even more pronounced as he gained weight, so
that in the last years he resembled a lumbering bear. I believed that he recognized me and that he remembered the
childhood we shared, the games we played, but I had no
proof except that he would let me lay a hand on his shoulder when we sat together and put my arms around his big
back when I said good-bye. We took walks around the
neighborhood and in a nearby park. Sometimes I helped
him with the chores he was assigned at the home. He had
been put in charge of the gardening, and as we walked
around the outside of the house I exclaimed over the birds
of paradise that were so plentiful and the twin Japanese
maple trees that flourished despite the heat. I was always
taken aback by the gentleness of his attentions toward the
garden when he plucked dead leaves from the ground or
straightened a stake. I could feel a familiar stab of hope as

I foolishly allowed myself to believe these ministrations indicated a satisfying life. Often during my visits he would become agitated. I had no power to calm him any longer, and when he was in a particular state, his caregivers would suggest I leave. They said they worried for my safety.

"Has my mother been here?" I asked the man.

"She was at the hospital, of course," he said. "She told us you would decide how to dispose of his remains."

"What?"

"Whether you prefer a burial or cremation. He had no will."

I had no ready answer. I had not expected to be confronted so boldly with the physical reality of my brother's death. My first reaction was anger at Laurel for not having dealt with this. It was typical of her careless and ultimately destructive optimism about my brother that she would not have thought ahead to a moment when this information would be necessary. It galled me that her idea of care did not extend to such an earthbound reality as death. But my anger was a futile and atavistic thing, and I realized, with a sadness even more dull than what I felt hearing the news of Malcolm's death—for that is what I felt, really, not shock at the unexpected heart attack of an overweight and inactive thirty-eight-year-old man, but a leaden sense of inevitability—that I did not know what my brother would have preferred. Despite the fact that my mother and I invented thought and desire for him, despite the fact that I folded him into my elaborate games as though he were a willing participant and imbued him with initiative when he had none, despite the fact that, even now, he remained as inseparable from me as my own guilty heart, neither one of us could have honestly said we knew what he wanted.

I slid open one of his dresser drawers and fingered a T-shirt. I was reminded of how huge his clothes had always been even when he was young and lank, how he preferred not to feel bound by cloth or touch. I imagined his bulk must have been an irritant for him, so much flesh defying his natural predilection for airiness. I wondered if he had continued to imagine flight.

The director handed me a shoebox. "Some things were in his desk," he said. "Not much. Nothing of value."

I had a strong reaction to this, as if the director were showing me Malcolm's dead body and not an old box, and I didn't immediately take it from his hands. After a moment, he put the box back on the desk. "Let me know what you decide about his remains," he said and left the room. I felt foolish sitting alone and left soon after.

Later, I checked into a motel and called Margaret. I felt grateful to hear the rough gravel of her voice. I imagined her hands, which she occasionally complained about, because her mother had been a hand model in Chicago and had made Margaret feel self-conscious about her body, which was powerful and athletic. Everything about Margaret's physicality was blunt and present. She stood as comfortably rooted to herself and her home as the mountains she loved. The strength of her lovemaking, which attracted me, also overwhelmed me so that I was sometimes relieved when we parted in the mornings, she for her job guiding climbers in the summer and skiers in the winter, and I for whatever seasonal work I picked up and the comforts of solitude. Still, Margaret was the first woman I had not fled from when the responsibilities of affection tightened around me and reminded me of the consequences of care. We had been together for a year and a half. I closed my eyes and saw her lake blue eyes, the smooth planes of her cheeks.

"How are you?" she asked.

"Hot. It's dry here."

She laughed. "You're ridiculous," she said affectionately. Her easy familiarity with my reticent nature still surprised me, and I had to work to ignore the discomfort being known engendered in me. She was frank in all things. She had made it clear early on that she would have none of my obfuscation. She wanted all of me or none of me, and for some reason, I took her at her word. I could not account for our longevity except to say that I found myself wanting to become necessary to her.

We were silent for a long time. I listened to her breath, remembered its natural sweetness, how it reminded me of the elusive scent of roses.

"I went to his room," I said, finally.

"Mmm."

"I sent his things to Goodwill."

"Your mother called right after you left."

I didn't respond.

"Have you spoken to her yet?" Margaret said.

"Not yet." During the drive I had imagined calling Laurel, had even pulled over at a rest stop at one point determined to do just that. But what would we say? We saw each other infrequently, perhaps once a year, and when we did, we cut wide swaths around what mattered. How could I talk about what it meant for Malcolm to be dead without stepping into a conversation I had avoided for so many years? Was Laurel prepared to hear the truth about the shooting? Was I prepared to tell it? What would happen when I let go of a lie I had held so long that it had become inextricable from my character?

"How did she sound?" I asked.

"Like she lost a son. When are you going to call her?"

I looked at the dresser, where the box full of Malcolm's things sat. "Did I ever tell you about Mal's treasures?" I said.

"You mean, along with all the other stories of your past you've regaled me with?" she said, her sarcasm light and forgiving.

I opened the lid. Inside lay a collection of rocks and sticks, an ace of diamonds, a golf tee, some coins, the plastic rings from a six-pack of soda, a bird feather. I couldn't speak for a few minutes. I felt ruined by what I saw. And then I described every object inside the box to Margaret. I was careful to explain how heavy a rock felt in my hand, to describe the specifics of its contours. I rubbed the feather against my face the way I knew Malcolm must have. Margaret listened and asked questions, too: What kind of bird did I think the feather came from? Was the rock igneous or sedimentary? I knew she cared about the answers, and I was grateful to her for honoring the importance of these random items. I could never understand what Malcolm saw in the orphaned bits and pieces he collected or why they were meaningful to him. I knew they didn't exactly explain or describe him. But I could believe he had made choices—this rock, not that one; this feather and not another—and that each object moved him in some way, and that he was capable of a kind of attachment, a very particular sort of love.

MALCOLM'S ASHES WEIGH SO LITTLE, like those plants my mother once loved, which were bleached and baked to a near unearthly lightness. Logic would dictate that we accrue weight along with years, but this turns out to be false. I understand science. I believe in it too, mostly, although there are things science can't easily explain. For instance: Why do some people go through life in groups, while others, like Malcolm, or Richard, or Kevin make their journeys alone? Or why does land root in your soul so that you feel you are not yourself when you are away from it? Do the qualities I see in this land around me, the equal parts of grace and despair, desolation and tenacity reflect something back to me that tells me who I am? Science has no answers for these questions. And although I have come to understand that my brother was born into the brain that steered him on his strange, foreshortened passage through life, and that a fall on a summer day so long ago did not de-

termine who he became, there is also a part of me that
knows that we drop each other and we pick each other up.
We do it over and over again.

A car drives up and parks at the edge of the beach.
Angelo and his wife and child get out. Angelo is tall like
his father and the only one of us who inherited our mother's red hair and fair skin. His boy runs down the beach,
and Angelo's young wife, heavy with their second child,
calls after him to be careful. Angelo raises a hand in greeting, and then my mother emerges from the car. She wears
a simple shift and sandals. A rope of heavy stones hangs
from her neck. Wooden bracelets circle her wrists. I
wonder if she ever missed that gold cross, and if she did,
what she imagined happened to it. She sees me, smiles and
waves.

I did call her from my motel room after I talked to Margaret. She answered the phone and said my name, as if she
had been waiting for me. I drove to see her that night.

She stayed in San Diego to be near Malcolm and to raise
Angelo, who was, to her dismay, a city boy, enamored of
noises and crowds. She took work at spas, and when that in-
dustry flourished so that there was barely a block in any
reasonable neighborhood that didn't boast some kind of es-
tablishment devoted to a new concept called "wellness," she
began her own. I still laugh to think of her running a business, no matter how small and homegrown hers is, and it is.
She rents a tumble-down cottage in a neighborhood that
was once marginal but now boasts gourmet food shops and
doggy daycare. She painted and salvaged until the place

took on a handmade, human quality that appeals to the kinds of people interested in her services. She pays her taxes and attends community board meetings. She lives above her business, and when I arrived that night she gave me a short tour of her spa rooms. They were typical and not much different from the rooms she worked in when I was young, except that I recognized her unique decorations—the walls and tabletops were festooned with her desert treasures.

We climbed the stairs to her second floor apartment and sat across from each other at her kitchen table. Her hair has turned grey, but she has never cut it short, and it falls about her shoulders like a magician's cape. Her face is finely wrinkled in a way that deepens her beauty. I was grateful for the mugs of tea that sent up a veil of steam between us. I did not know how to begin. I never told her the truth about what happened the day of Kevin's death, and this information, held for so many years, has widened the distance between us. When I was younger, the secret felt like the necessary repository of my anger toward her, and I withheld the truth with all the self-righteous spite of any young man who defines himself in opposition to what he does not wish to become. That night, I was determined to tell her the simple truth: that Malcolm had shot Kevin and that I had carried that secret for thirty years, but that I no longer would or could. I had allowed it to shape me, to become the myth I based my life on, but that it was just that: a fairy story I told myself in order to survive my particular war. I was done with all that now.

But as the steam cleared and I looked into her face, I said nothing. What would the truth do to us now? How would it change us? Would it open us up to regret and recrimination? Would it serve to separate us from each other forever? Staring at my mother, so lovely in her years, I did not want that.

"I miss him already," she said. "My sweet, dear Malcolm."

And so I said nothing. Her love for Malcolm was uncritical even to the end, and I believed that he deserved such devotion. I believe we all do, but it is the rare ones among us who are lucky enough to receive it. My brother was lucky. Sitting in that room, my hands around the warm mug, watching her eyes sparkle with barely restrained tears, I knew that I was lucky, too.

"GRANDMA! LOOK!"

Angelo's son jumps up and down, and Laurel meets him at the shore, bending to inspect something the sea has brought in. When she stands, he reaches his arms up, and she lifts him onto her hip. They are easy with each other. He leans his head on her shoulder and takes a piece of her hair into his hands, rubbing the ends against his cheek. I can tell this is their habit, and that it comforts them both.

Angelo meets me by the shoreline. He looks at the murky water, and I know from his expression that if he feels anything for this place that was never his home it is only the kind of disconnected interest we summon when our parents describe the haunts and follies of their childhoods. This place is not his history. What happened here is the story of strangers. Still, I wish I could make him see how it was when Malcolm was a boy and stood by this sea, how he crouched to study something no one else would take the time to notice, how he jumped up and down in excitement at a passing flock of birds. I wish I could make Angelo hear the pitch-perfect caw that Malcolm made, a sound so uncannily right that for one moment he became indistinguishable from the birds he loved so much.

Laurel walks over to us and transfers her grandson to his father's arms. She reaches up and touches my cheek. Her finger traces the line of my jaw. I remember her hands running over the spines of plants, feeling them as a way of knowing them. Her eyes travel down to the box in my hand. Her expression seizes as she registers what is inside.

"I'm sorry," I tell her, remembering the times she said these same words to me, as if my mistakes were her fault, and as if she understood the inevitable complications of my future but wanted, against all logic, to relieve me of their weight. I think I mean these words in the same way. I wonder if my heart is big enough to carry her burdens as she did mine.

There are things we might say to each other about innocence and guilt, about grievous mistakes and their consequences, about the punishing ramifications of willful ignorance. But we are trapped by history. Knowledge cannot change who we were and what we did to each other.

Was Malcolm guilty of murder? I've thought about this question nearly every day of my life. Did he act out of rage or love? Did he know he was taking one life to save another? I ask myself, too, if I need answers to these questions. Are there any words that will tell me what I want to know?

ABOUT THE AUTHOR

Marisa Silver is the author of *Babe in Paradise,* a collection of short stories, and the novel *No Direction Home.* She made her fictional debut in *The New Yorker,* and her work has been anthologized in *The Best American Short Stories.* She lives in Los Angeles.

MAY 02 —